The end of the world as we know it.

Lesley Choyce

Red Deer PRESS

Published by Red Deer Press
A Fitzhenry & Whiteside Company
1512, 1800 – 4 Street SW
Calgary AB T2S 2S5
www.reddeerpress.com
www.fitzhenry.ca

CREDITS
Edited for the Press by Peter Carver
Copyedited by Kirstin Morrell
Cover design by Duncan Campbell
Text design by Jacquie Morris
Cover image courtesy Diane White Rosie/iStockphoto
Printed and bound in Canada by Friesens for Red Deer Press

ACKNOWLEDGEMENTS
Red Deer Press acknowledges the support of the Canada Council for the Arts, which
last year invested $20.1 million in writing and publishing throughout Canada.
Financial support also provided by Government of Canada through the Book
Publishing Industry Development Program (BPIDP).

Canada Council   Conseil des Arts
for the Arts   du Canada

Canada

Library and Archives Canada Cataloguing in Publication

Choyce, Lesley, 1951–
The end of the world as we know it / Lesley Choyce.

ISBN 978-0-88995-379-6

I. Title.

PS8555.H668E56 2007   jC813'.54   C2007-901661-8

Dedication

For all of my students over the years
and the lessons they taught me

Chapter One

I hate the world and everything in it.

That's the way I began my personal essay for English. Mr. Dodd, with great enthusiasm, had told us, "I want you to write something that is true, something that expresses who you really are. No holds barred. Spill it right out. Hold nothing back. Write something that comes from deep within you and expresses your inner truth. That is what language is for." By this point, he was staring up at the stippled ceiling. His chin was pointed outward, his arms behind his back. He somehow reminded me of a bird. It must have been the thrust of his Adam's apple that made me think of a buzzard I'd seen once disembowelling a dead animal by the side of the road.

I was in a black mood—a fairly permanent condition in my life. So I spilled it out just as he asked.

I hate the world and everything in it. I realize this is a big generalization but it is true. It means that I hate this school, I hate the people in it, I hate the country I live in, and I hate my parents. I hate you, Mr. Dodd, even though, as you can see, you should not take this personally because my feelings are all-inclusive. Of course, I hate Farnsworth Academy. I mean, look at this dump. I also hate the weather. Even when it is sunny and warm. I hate all four seasons, none more so than the others. There is a perfect democratic notion to the way I feel. You must begin to see this is true. I hate the way we live and the things that people do.

All you have to do is turn on the news and see why hating the world is a perfectly logical response. People who are happy in this world are just faking it or making it up. It's possible that I am the only honest person in this ridiculous institution that pretends to be a school. Honest, clear-thinking individuals like me down through history are persecuted, I know that. Those of my tribe have been burned at the stake, beheaded (my personal favorite), tortured with inventive, excruciatingly painful hardware, shackled and left to die in dungeons, drowned, buried alive, and, in any number of other ways, terminally punished. This, however, does not scare me or deter me from expressing my own feelings.

I hate the world and everything in it. And that includes me.

Mr. Dodd must have read my essay that afternoon while I was sitting in study hall picking at a scab on my elbow. He tracked me down where I sat on the big, stuffed leather sofa by the fireplace in the library and dropped the paper in my lap.

"You gave me an *A*?"

"It was impressive, Carson. Dr. Cromwell would like to see you."

Dr. Cromwell was the man who ran this private school for screwups that we like to call Flunk Out Academy. He was trained as a psychologist, or so he said. My own estimation was that he was both insane and inventive and had somehow blundered on a role that suited him well—headmaster of an expensive private high school for messed-up kids. His accent was fake British. He was from here but he claimed that his days at Cambridge and Oxford had given him the accent. Cromwell was a tall, thin man with one of those round bellies that made him look like he was either hiding a basketball under his academic robes (yes, he actually wore a kind of academic gown daily) or he was pregnant. He had a face that told you he had suffered serious acne while he was a boy and had been ridiculed by his peers. (I also hated my own peers, by the way—pretty well hated them all.) But it was Cromwell's eyes that told you he was criminally insane. He drilled right through you and made you believe he was trying to hypnotize you or control your mind. But it was all a kind of put-on, something theatrical, like the Brit accent.

Although I hated Cromwell as much as the next creature on the planet, I found him entertaining and a bit of a challenge. I don't think he was as smart as he pretended to be and certainly he was not as smart as I was, but he had his charm. There was something endearing about his mind games that I liked.

"Professor Dodd . . . " (he called all the teachers "professor") " . . . has shown me your paper. Congratulations on the A."

"I deserved it."

"The other students apparently wrote about more mundane things." I could tell by the tone of his voice that Cromwell was on one of his famous fishing expeditions.

"Like?" I smacked the little ball back over to his side of the net.

A flick of the fingers on each hand out to the side. A transitional ("Give me a minute to remember," it meant) downturn of the mouth. "Horses. One of your classmates wrote about how she felt about horses."

I rolled my eyes. "And?"

"Hockey, I believe. Another on flowers."

"Did Code-X write about drugs? Did he write about which ones were his favorites again?"

"I didn't read them all."

"But you singled out mine for this discussion?"

"Yes. Yours was the most . . . interesting."

"That's why Professor Doodle turned me in, right?" I decided to play smart-ass for his and my own amusement.

"He didn't turn you in, Carson. He expressed concern."

• • •

There was a pause in the conversation just then, so it seems like a good time to fill you in about this place. Farnsworth Academy. Rich-ass, screwed-up kids like me ended up here. Some pretended it was a place of privilege. I contended it was a holding tank for future psychos whose parents happened to have the big bucks. One of the requirements to get admission to this school, as devised by Dr. Cromwell himself, was that you must have been kicked out of or flunked out of at least three schools prior to this. Hence, Flunk Out Academy, as we called it. Because we came from well-off families, we were all beautiful losers (as some would say)—though I didn't know about the beautiful part. It was an ugly, hateful world and we were part of it. I was one of the few who saw it as it truly was.

The establishment itself was an old, run-down (and I do mean dilapidated, boys and girls) mansion that was once the home of some greedy tycoon who owned two asbestos mines where he employed immigrant laborers who all died of hideous diseases as a reward for their labor. Cromwell bought the crumbling edifice at a bargain basement price with the promise he would tear it down, but instead he opened up this private school. The plaques on his wall suggested he did have a PhD in psychology from Oxford but I was willing to bet you could buy those things over the Internet.

• • •

Cromwell waited for me to do something during the pause. Anything would have been meaningful and worthy of his interpretation. I could have belched, farted, moaned loudly, or started to hum the French national anthem. I chose silence as my current coping mechanism. Even that caused him to raise eyebrows. "So what do you think?" he continued.

"About what?" I could see the worm dangling on the hook but I really wasn't that hungry.

"This thing about hate?"

"As I understand it, adults think 'hate' is a powerful word, a nasty word. Am I safe to assume this?"

"You are."

"Look, Dr. Crom, I don't use the word lightly. P. Doodle wanted something honest and I thought I showed him a great deal of respect for coming out and writing what was really true. Do you understand how rare that is in this big, convoluted, hideous world?" I wanted to use the F-word in there but did not, which really puzzled me. Was I losing my edge, trying to be polite? That would be scary.

"Honesty is not always praised in this century, I agree. Perhaps you and I can change that?"

I let out one of those horse sounds. Air rushing out between my lips. "Name the goddam century that rewarded honesty," I demanded.

"The fourteenth," he said without blinking an eyelash.

"If I'm correct, didn't the bubonic plague kill off half the population of Europe around 1350?"

"'Tis true. There were a few rough patches. But, despite the punishment of nature, there was strong ethical upwelling. There were many who believed in a code of honor."

"I'll keep that little morsel of information in my back pocket in case I need it. Thanks for the enlightenment."

Another pause while Dr. C. made a little castle with his fingers and touched his lips.

"All I'd like you to consider, if you will, is the *source* of your hatred, your anger."

"Hey, I didn't write anything about being angry. It's all about hatred pure and simple, as a logical response to the world as it is." Why couldn't he see the difference?

"Okay. Okay." His fingers created a bridge in front of him, London Bridge to be exact, before it was taken apart and shipped to Arizona. "Just try to identify the origins of the hatred, the sources. We are your allies here, not your enemies."

I wanted to say, *With allies like you, who needs enemies*? But it would have sounded like a line from a bad movie and I hate how movies portray real life. "Are we through?" I asked.

"I don't know. Are we?"

I gave him a don't-squeeze-the-merchandise look and left. I did not slam the door on the way out.

Chapter Two

The students at Farnsworth Academy lived there most of the time. That way we didn't have to deal with our parents and they didn't have to deal with us. The amazing thing about sweet FA (if this was a university, it would be FU) was that no one was ever booted out of here. A kid dropped dynamite into the fish pond and killed all of Dr. Crom's pet goldfish, some over ten years old, and he didn't get kicked out. Ryan Luger, or Code-X as he liked to be called, had been busted for possession of weed, car theft, and even identity theft, but he was still here. Apparently there was no way out of here except graduation. It was that scary.

I would tell you about my parents but there is really not much to say. I'm sure I was a big disappointment to them. And I started out with so much promise. Piano lessons, science projects involving moving parts, Scouts. I was a voracious reader and still am, but apparently now I read all the wrong books. I was once even a daydreamer with "healthy" daydreams. All the etceteras. But I changed. It was my only option really when it sunk in what kind of a planet I had been born on.

I didn't blame my parents. They tried their best. I had an intellectual awakening, although that may sound funny when I put it down like that. I believed I had learned how to see things as they really are. Some kids say, quite naively, life sucks and then you die. I thought it was worse than that. I only wished it could have been that simple.

• • •

When I moved in here, I was assigned a roommate. Griffin Fitzgerald. GFG as some call him. I called him Fin and he seemed to like me calling him that. Fin was pale and that's what everyone noticed first. His nose ran most of the time and he sniffled. He wore white shirts and black pants with a crease in them. We didn't have uniforms although they tried that once. Gilbert Dean, our resident pyromaniac, collected all the uniforms one weekend three years before and made a lovely pyre down by the fish pond late on a Saturday night. Dr. Cromwell decided he couldn't afford to replace them so we went back to what Crom called "never ending casual days."

Fin hoped to one day build nuclear weapons. He was saddened by what he heard in the news about the possible dwindling of nuclear arsenals. But he knew that there was a heck of a lot of enriched uranium piling up out there, and more where that came from, so he had hope for the future—at least the future of his own career. Fin was here because he was caught at his public school downloading files about how to make a "suitcase nuclear weapon," and making inquiries through chat rooms about where he could get his hands on some "cheap" uranium to make what they call a "dirty" nuclear device. Had he been left unhindered,

Fin would have had the smarts and the financial resources (by way of tapping into his parents' bank account) to actually make this happen and the world might have come to its knees. At least that was the way Fin told it.

Even though I hated Fin, my weird roommate, along with all the rest of the vile human conglomerate, I admit that I admired him a little. Unlike me who sat back honing my malevolence against the world, Fin had actually worked on a plan towards ending the world as we know it. And you've got to give the kid kudos for that.

Although almost none of us other than Fin had plans for our futures, some of us would soon be finished at Farnsworth and tossed back into the rotting cabbage patch of humanity. I was almost seventeen and finishing up my third year. Another year in this hellhole and then . . . well, then, I didn't know. I really didn't.

Fin, on the other hand, knew he needed more education. He was bright after all. He planned to go to university to study physics, then work his way up in the nuclear industry if there was still anything left of it. He and I made fun of all the do-gooders who wanted to end the arms race. Fortunately, there were powerful men with lots of money who wanted to put weapons into space, nukes even, and that had to be a good thing, at least from a career point of view, for a guy like Fin.

Although I had no need or desire for friends, Fin had confessed that he considered me his friend and ally. (Remember my thoughts on allies.) Fin tried to be helpful when I was in one of my dark moods. I was not easy to be around when I was in a dark mood. Sometimes I would skip class. Sometimes I would sleep. Sometimes I would lie in bed and feel like I was about to explode with the rage inside me, although I would never give Dr. Crumbs the satisfaction of telling him how angry I got.

Although many of us should have been in jail or other constrictive institutions, we had considerable freedom here at FOA and wandered down into the small town of Harborville whenever we pleased. Harborville has a main drag with a few stores, a pub, a post office, a liquor store, an abandoned movie theater, and not much else of significance except for a used bookstore run by an old man named Mel, who looked like he stepped out of a really bad old movie.

None of the kids from the school came from Harborville (or Hooterville as we sometimes called it). We were stuck in the heart of Farmer Clem country and it was peopled by men and women who actually grew apples and raised chickens and walked around town with cow shit stuck to their boots. We made fun of them for being hicks, but some kids, I think, secretly wished they had grown up with Jed and Granny Clampett as their family. I didn't share that feeling, of course. I had little interest in these folksy types who stood around the IGA store and discussed weather and tides. I thought of them as background noise and prop visuals when I walked downtown. I always went alone and tried hard not to make eye contact with anyone. I didn't even know why I wandered down there except to look at the water in the harbor and peer deep into it while sitting on the town wharf. If I stared at the dark water long enough, everything seemed to disappear and I felt like I was far away from everything . . . me included. And that, to be honest, felt good.

Afterwards, I sometimes went into Mel's used bookstore, and if Mel had been drinking (I think his passion was rum but it could have been brandy), he would argue with me about medieval torture or the history of war, or any one of the morbid subjects in which we shared an interest.

Mel was about fifty, I think, and he didn't give a rat's ass as to what the people of H'ville thought about him. He called them Harborvillains sometimes and he referred to the town as Heartlessville. Sometimes he called the inhabitants the People of the Turds, because they were farmers and spread shredded cow-pies on their fields at various times of the year. Mel had had more years than me to work at the craft of despising humanity and I looked up to him for that. I introduced him once to Fin and they spoke for nearly an hour about what a nuclear attack would really be like. Fin especially was entranced with Mel's description of skin melting off your body if you were just at the right distance from ground zero.

Mel cultivated a dishevelled look: shirt not tucked in, unshaven, glasses askew. The end of his belt dangled and sometimes he'd forget to zip up his khaki pants, although I don't think he was a perv or anything. He had focused much of his energy on the study of how heinous mankind was and was well-versed beyond my wildest dreams.

"Genghis Khan," he muttered as an introduction one day when I arrived looking for a safe haven free of Hootervillains and the rest of the cow crap populace, "Genghis Khan said—and I quote from memory: 'Happiness lies in overcoming your enemies, in seizing their property, in savoring their agony, and in outraging their wives and daughters.' Remember that, Carson Sullivan. Remember that there was one man honest enough to speak it clearly and let it be known. Genghis Khan had no need to gussy it up with fancy beliefs or rhetoric or flags or self-importance."

Mel sipped from a coffee cup that I eventually figured out was real coffee diluted with real rum (or brandy, or both). He had offered me a taste on occasion but I'd declined and I never quite knew why. I think I was afraid that it contained saliva. I've never been a fan of other people's saliva.

I was not kind to Mel and he was one of the rare few who appreciated my version of candor. "This place looks like a pigsty, Mel. What will your customers think?"

"If they can't accept me and my store as it is, I don't give a rat's ass." Mel didn't give a rat's ass about any number of things: appearances, Hootervillains, the news, money, laws. Even laws of physics. Once, in a rare talkative mood, I told Mel that I thought that one of the best things that could happen to us all was to wake up one morning and discover that gravity had ceased to exist; then we would all spin off into deep space and nothingness.

"You think I care about gravity?" he said. He shook his head in a way that indicated he didn't give one hair off the rat's ass of concern with gravity. You could compress the entire known universe into a couple of molecules in a black hole, somewhere ten thousand light years away, and it wouldn't bother him.

Nothing much really did bother Mel as he explained it, although he seemed rather exercised on many issues on many occasions. It seemed the less concerned he claimed to be about anything, the more he wanted to discuss it. It was my job to get him going. "What would you be, Mel, if you weren't a bookseller?"

"Nothing else," he would say. "Bookselling is the highest profession. I'm a guardian of the truth, no matter how hideous it may be. The right books lay history bare. Had I my druthers, though, I would have lived in another time, perhaps as a soldier in an army led by someone like Genghis Khan or, better yet, Attila the Hun."

"The Huns were really cool," I'd say, just to get him going.

"Attila was known as 'the Scourge of God.' That was some moniker. He ruled from the Alps to the Caspian Sea and assaulted the Roman Empire. He would have been responsible for the deaths of thousands if not millions of men. Sadly, he died of overindulgence at his wedding feast when he was a mere forty-seven. A great, glowing flame . . . out and gone forever." He shook his head, tried to tuck his belt back into a loop in his pants, and wiped at a bit of drool escaping from the corner of this mouth. "We live in a very dark age," he announced at length.

Chapter Three

I had been a student at Farnsworth since the fall. I'd lasted one whole week of September in my old high school until they finally gave me the boot. I already had a bad reputation for talking back to teachers, walking out of class whenever I wanted to, acting like a smart-ass with the guidance counsellor and the vice principal. The trouble was I knew I was smarter than they all were and I think they knew it. And it was obvious that the vast majority of students back at that public hellhole were assholes. Sometimes I'd lose my cool if someone looked at me the wrong way and I'd call them that to their ugly faces.

My final trio of crimes back at Hellhole High went like this. Dennis Welch wrenched open his locker beside me in the hall and the door hit me hard in the shoulder. He didn't say he was sorry. He didn't say anything. I called him a shithead and a human parasite. He called me a hemorrhoid—which, coming from Dennis, was rather creative. But it still pissed me off. So I spit on him. Not in his face, just on his shirt. And then I walked away.

Needless to say, I ended up in the office, and I was up

against the principal this time. He was a man I despised. I could see in his eyes that the feeling was reciprocal.

"Carson, what the hell is your problem?" he began.

"You are my problem, Jeffrey," I said. "You and the lowlife scum that infest the hallways of this place." I don't know why I made the leap of calling him by his first name but it somehow helped level the playing field—or so I thought.

He seethed. I almost thought he might hit me. Which would have been a victory of sorts. But he didn't. "You have a total lack of respect for me or anything about this school, don't you?"

"That's a fair observation, Jeffrey."

He was trying to reign in his anger. "Don't address me by my first name, Carson."

"What do you want me to call you? Jerk-off?"

He said nothing. Instead, he called in the vice principal and then left the room. My fate was sealed.

• • •

I don't think you could say I was well-liked at Farnsworth. I was not particularly kind to anyone and the best I could muster was benign tolerance, the sort of thing that allowed me to bunk in a room with Griffin Fitzgerald. Along with my poor social skills, I fell short in a number of other areas as well. My parents and teachers and Dr. Crumbles had come up with various lists of things I should have been interested in. I'd hate to bore you with the full list but the synopsis goes like this:

I should be interested in my future.

I should be interested in my school work.

I should be interested in the well-being of others.

I should be interested in things that other kids my age were interested in.

I should be interested in girls.

I was, after all, sixteen, nearly seventeen and going on forty. I was old beyond my years, as I saw it. I think I could have been interested in girls if the right one came along but there seemed fat chance of that. Here's an example of the way I related to the opposite sex.

In class one day, Marinda (whose mother was an anorexic Euro model) said out loud, "Mr. Dodd, do I have to sit by Carson again?"

Mr. Dodd replied, "What's wrong with sitting by Carson?"

"He wears the same clothes every day and I don't think he bathes."

"Bitch," I said.

"Carson, I won't have that language in this class."

"Female dog," I corrected myself.

"This is unacceptable," Marinda said. This from a girl who was thrown out of not three but five schools in total.

Mr. Dodd suggested that we should have a peer counselling session regarding the bad feelings between Marinda and myself.

It was Code-X (Ryan) who first suggested where Mr. Doodle should insert his peer-counselling session.

Oddly enough, I was attracted to Marinda—at least to Marinda's body, which was quite extraordinary. Dr. Cromwell—and a pair of real professional counsellors from before he came on the scene—had told me that I had a problem relating to girls and women. This was sheer genius on their part, since I had a problem with everyone. Females make up—what?—fifty-five percent of the human race, so all that high-powered education went to telling me I was "tending towards misogyny," and needed (surprise, surprise) counselling.

To finish the Marinda conversation, it went like this. "Maybe I should just move to another seat," I offered. It was just a ploy. I wasn't trying to be helpful or nice. And I did "bathe," as she called it. And I did have several sets of clothes but they were all the same. Black T-shirt, black pants, black sweater over top hanging down to my knees. It looked like I was in mourning, some would say. But it was not that.

"Marinda, maybe you should apologize for hurting Carson's feelings." Tables turned.

"Apologize?"

"Please," Mr. D. requested.

"It would help," I said, trying to hold back a sinister laugh.

"But he's just so . . . so . . ."

I was disappointed she didn't finish. She was crying now. I had that effect on girls, which probably explains why I would be no good in a relationship. Instead, Code-X and Mary Partridge decided it was a kind of fill-in-the-blank game.

"Gross?" Coder suggested.

"Scummy," Mary added. (Mary, who had her own weight and personal hygiene issues.)

"Grotesque?"

"Disgusting?"

"Despicable?"

"Obscene?"

Mr. Dodd could see that peer counselling was not working out the way they said it would in his university education classes. "Enough is enough," he said. "I will apologize for this myself, Carson. I truly am sorry."

"No problem," I said. I was really pretty cool with all the insults. I'd weathered worse. My shell was like that of a Galapagos tortoise. You needed some truly high-powered ammunition and a gun with a big kick if anything was going to bust through that armament. Besides, these were my classmates. I'd been kicked around by nastier louts than these. These were my peeps, my homies. I could take a little teasing now and then.

After class, I asked Marinda with her short, short skirt, "Are those your real legs or just two hockey sticks going from your shoes up to your hips?"

She gave me a look that could have nuked the Pentagon, then fled to her room with her roommate, Giselle, trying to pick up her books and notes as she left. I stood my ground as Giselle addressed me with fiery eyes and a muffled voice, "Carson, you'll get what you deserve."

• • •

I returned to my room to pick up my history textbook and realized that the words were probably true. I would get what I deserved. We all would. It was the kind of Pavlovian, Darwinian world we lived in. Reaping what we sow. Like the farmers outside Hooterville, the People of the Turds, planting and harvesting their crops. I had little hope for happiness in my life. I pitied those who expected to be happy, those who expected to do good deeds, work hard, and then "get what they deserve."

Life, alas, did not simply suck and then give way to demise. We were all being punished with the pain of living for some sins we could not even comprehend. It was a one-way ticket fraught with many unpleasant stops along the way.

In order to escape from my peers, I took a quick trip into the kitchen, where Mrs. Chin was cooking spaghetti. Mrs. Chin, I think, liked me. Without speaking she made me a peanut butter and grape jelly sandwich, and put it on a small plate. She poured me a glass of Dr. Pepper from her own personal stash. I ate quietly at the kitchen counter seated on a bar stool. When I finished, she smiled at me and I almost thanked her but couldn't quite bring myself to do it. I'm pretty sure she understood why.

• • •

Back in my room, Fin was on the net again. "Where's Uzbekistan?" he asked.

"One of the old Soviet spin-offs. South of Siberia, maybe? Near Pakistan? Why?"

"Just wondering," he said. "I've got a lead on some material. It's probably just a ruse, though."

"Material" meant "fissionable material" in Fin's world. "What's the asking price?"

"Two mill US."

"Upfront?"

"Seems so."

"Gonna go for it?"

"If it sounds too good to be true, it probably is. I'll have to pass."

"That's what I'd do," I said. "Tomorrow is another day."

• • •

I decided to skip history. We were reading about the founding of the League of Nations, an attempt to create a peaceful, cooperative world that failed. I figured I had better things to do with my time. I knew that I would not really get in trouble for cutting class. At worst, I'd end up in Cromwell's office for a lecture. I needed some fresh air, so I said, "Happy hunting," to Fin and went down the hallway past the old paintings of dead rich men. The sun was out, which surprised me, and it was warmer than expected. I walked for a bit and was shocked to find myself thinking about Marinda, thinking about her rather attractive face and then the tears. What was that all about anyway? The crying routine? I was sure I'd never understand girls.

A vehicle was approaching from behind and I put out my thumb. A hayseed in an old truck stopped.

"From the academy, eh?"

"Yes, sir."

"A fine place, they say."

"As fine as they get."

"Learn anything important today?"

"You betcha."

"That's what education is all about, lad."

I looked in the back of the truck and saw it was filled with various engine parts—from a tractor maybe. He noticed that I had noticed. "Had to tear the damn thing down piece by bloody piece until I found out what was wrong. Turned out to be a bent rod. Got a new one. Now the hard part is puttin' 'er back together."

He dropped me off by the wharf as I requested and it was empty. The tide was low and the boats floated well below the dock. I found my favorite spot near the end and sat down beside an old, tired-looking but wary seagull that had employed his leisure time well by crapping white seagull poop all over the weathered planks beneath him. I stared down into the dark water as I had done many times before and imagined there was another world down there, a better place than this one, a world where things made sense and where history did not exist. A place where I did not exist.

• • •

I sometimes wondered what would become of all of us once we left Flunk Out Academy. Cromwell was a benevolent dictator of sorts. It was Mel Watson, my esteemed, inebriated mentor from the bookstore, who pointed out the similarity (or was it irony?) of the headmaster's name. Mel had a mind like a bear trap when it came to holding onto anything about military slaughter and organized annihilation. That was part of what I liked about him. He should have been teaching history himself at a school or university. Instead, he drank rum in Tim Horton's coffee and ran a bookstore. I had never heard of Oliver Cromwell but Mel was well-versed on the dead Englishman.

"Between 1653 and 1658, Cromwell was Lord Protector of England, Ireland, and Scotland. Now there's a role to live up to. The question was, what was he protecting? He had already led massacres against his many opponents in Ireland and Scotland. When he rose to power, he claimed to be protecting the people from King Charles I. He ended up having the King's head—lopped, that is. Cromwell became himself a kind of dictator and did little good. Military men make poor politicians. History is full of such splendid madness, though.

"All the spilled blood of history eventually seeps back into the earth. Did you know that, Carson?" Mel took off those gnomish, round, metal-rim glasses and polished them on his coffee/rum- (or maybe it was brandy-) stained shirt. "The best of us come into this world, wreak as much havoc as we can, and then pass on into nothingness. 'Tis the way it is."

More cheerful thoughts to ponder. And ponder I did, as I sat at the end of the Harborville wharf waiting for something, anything, to happen. I was one of those in the select club of humans, who, if told that the world would end tomorrow, would shrug and go about my business, which is to say, I wouldn't particularly care. I would maybe eat a hamburger with greasy french fries, down a Pepsi, and then take a nap. I had already adjusted my sights on the possibility of a tomorrow-less world.

At the land-end of the wharf, a truck had stopped and two men in overalls got out and began complaining about gas prices and taxes. Their truck was idling noisily and they had the radio playing an appalling song about honky-tonks and patriotism. It really fouled the mood I was working on. Dwelling on the end of the world and nothingness can be really disrupted by bad country music and a couple of hicks with nothing better to do than exercise their vocal chords. I was watching them with disdain when I noticed a girl walk past them. She had long, dark hair that had been dyed a kind of—what was it, anyway?—henna reddish. She wore a shredded T-shirt with the words *Eat the Rich* and low-slung, hip-hugger pants with an inch of skin showing above.

The rural complainers studied her in a lewd way as she walked past them but she didn't seem to notice. I'd seen her around town maybe once before. She was a local for sure, probably someone from the trailer park, a welfare kid most likely. I'd never seen her down here at the wharf before, though.

She walked right past me as if I was invisible. She went right to the end and stood there staring off into space. I confess that I found myself staring at her ass. That sight was the best thing that had happened to me all day. I wondered what she was looking at, but figured that, like me, she was just staring at nothing in particular. Maybe she was waiting for aliens to beam her up to the mothership. It looked like that kind of scene. She just stood there doing nothing.

I heard the truck doors close and the engine gunned as the farm boys drove off, undoubtedly to pick up where they left off spreading cow poo over the fertile fields outside Hooterville.

That's when the girl let out this high-pitched, god-awful shriek. I'd never heard anything like it. Even though we were outside, it was deafening. I sat stone still not knowing what to do. I looked back towards town but no one was in the vicinity. My gut reaction was to get the hell out of there lest I got accused of provoking or attacking her. I wanted to retreat to the safe oblivion of my room back at Farnsworth. I started to get up to leave.

She turned around suddenly and looked right at me. "Where the hell are you going?" she asked with venom in her voice. Her eyes were dark as coal and she had a kind of ghoulish mascara that made them seem even darker. She had one of those little silver balls planted on her pierced tongue. There was defiance written all over her.

"I'm just leaving, okay? You can stay and scream all you like. I don't care."

I started to walk away, shaking my head. So much for my wharf-side asylum of peace and quiet. I began to walk fast and I think I must have heard her begin to run towards me but kept pretending that nothing was happening. That's when I felt her kick me once and then twice in the back of each knee until I crumpled onto the boards. Man, did that ever hurt.

She just stood there, over me, like she'd done nothing at all, like I tripped or something. "Freak," I said—apparently the best insult I could come up with, although it felt a tad too tame as soon as I said it.

She kicked me again. Only this time I grabbed her foot. I held on tight and didn't let go. She tried to kick again but I lifted her leg and it caused her to fall. She fell hard.

"Damn you," she said.

"Who the hell do you think you are?"

"Oh, I know who I am," she said. "Now let go."

I suddenly realized that I was shaking. What the hell was it with this crazy girl? I took a chance and let go of her leg. She involuntarily reached for her ankle. I must have hurt her. That's when I noticed the marks on her arms. Again, I had this feeling that I should just turn and run, get as far away from her as I could as quick as I could. But I didn't do that.

"You gonna scream again?"

"I didn't scream," she said.

"I heard you. You walked to the end of the wharf and just let out a screech. It scared the shit out of me. Are you, like, insane or what?" I couldn't believe I was having a conversation with this freaked-out girl.

"Oh, that," she said, suddenly letting down her guard. "It's the only thing that helps."

I was looking at her arms again, both of them. Scars. Wounds healed, some scabbed over. Not needles, not drugs. Something else. I didn't want to get involved. I stood up to leave. "Nice getting to know you," I said, brushing off my pants.

She was still sitting down. "Do you really want to know what I was doing?" she asked.

"No, I don't," I said. "And I don't care." I had enough complications in my life and this girl had big problems. Distance was my plan as I hobbled away.

She got up and ran to me. I waited for my knees to buckle again but didn't turn around. Instead, she touched me. She grabbed my arm and held onto it, walking beside me. I was afraid to look over at her but when I did, I saw the look of a deranged person in her eyes. I'd seen that look somewhere before and didn't want to own up to it, but there it was.

I'd seen that look in the mirror. More than once.

"What I was doing," she insisted, "was trying to let the pain escape. I was pushing it out. I was getting rid of it. If I didn't do that I'd lose it altogether. I'd go crazy."

I wanted to tell her she was already crazy. I wanted to tell her to go live her own messed-up life and leave me out of it.

"Do you know how much I hate this stupid town?" she asked.

She was still making me plenty nervous but I let my guard down just a little. "Join the club."

"There's a club?"

At first I didn't catch on that it was a joke. Then she squeezed my arm harder. I stopped and looked at her. "What do you want?" I asked, putting up my defences.

"I want to find one freaking thing in this town that I don't hate. Anything. Can you help me do that?"

I suddenly realized how bad my legs hurt. There was an excruciating pain behind my knees. I wondered if she had snapped tendons or something. I yanked my arm away from her grasp but she kept looking at me. I was about to just run. I really was. But she was staring at me. I'd never seen a girl who scared me so much.

The next thing I knew, I grabbed her arm. I think I hurt her. I could feel the scars, the scabs where something had cut her. She didn't resist. I walked her back out on the wharf a ways and then took her to the edge. "Look," I said. "Look down there at that."

It was just dark water and long fronds of seaweed undulating back and forth in the surge of the water like long, flowing hair. It wasn't just the water or the seaweed; it was the place I would go to when nothing else would help. She started to look away but I held her arm and made her keep looking down. "Do you hate that?" I asked, almost shouting. Who was the deranged one now?

She looked intently downward and then took a deep breath. And then another. She tried to pull her arm away again but then stopped. "No," she said. "I don't hate that."

Chapter Four

Her name was Christine, although she said she hated her name and had tried to come up with something she liked better but failed. After she sat and stared at the water for maybe five minutes, she stood up, somewhat transformed. That is to say, she was no longer violent. "Follow me," she said.

"No way," I said. Why should I follow her? This girl was nothing but trouble with a capital T. I had this odd, bizarre longing to be back "home," home in this case being my room back in the dilapidated mansion of Farnsworth Academy with my feet up and the clicking sound of the keyboard as Fin sought inside info on stolen plutonium or enriched uranium in various unpronounceable parts of the planet.

"Okay," she said. "I can take a hint." But, as she was walking away, I had this sudden curiosity. I needed to see what would happen next.

"Wait," I said. All I could muster was a fast limp as I tried to catch up with her.

• • •

We didn't talk at all as we walked away from the harbor and uphill on a road leading out of town. The stately, larger homes of downtown Harborville gave way to more broken-down, paint-chipped houses with car wrecks in the front yard. The real estate kept declining in value until we finally came to the Green Valley Trailer Park, a place I'd heard about but never had the slightest interest in visiting. There were no trees here as they'd all been bulldozed to provide maximum room for cramming as many mobile homes into the space available. There were narrow gravel lanes with many potholes filled with brown water. A couple of stray dogs walked around pissing on tires as if they owned the place. "Check out the street names," Christine said.

"Sleepy Lane? You've got to be kidding." There were handmade wooden street signs on rusty metal posts at every corner.

"It gets worse." She pointed towards Sneezy Lane, Doc Avenue, and Lazy Boulevard. Then she pointed further up the hill. "And my personal favorite—ta-da!"

I squinted until I could make it out. "Dopey Drive."

She shrugged. "The creep who owns this place has a thing for Snow White and the Seven Dwarfs."

"Do people actually say they live on Dopey Drive?"

"If you live on Dopey Drive, it's part of your address whether you like it or not."

I noticed now that some of the aging, run-down trailers actually had little wooden paintings of Snow White or one of the favored dwarfs planted on sticks in their front yards—if you could call hard-packed, tire-rutted, lifeless clay a front yard.

"How long have you lived here?" I asked.

"Forever. Forever and then some. You want to hear my story?"

"No. I hate it when people want to tell me their life stories."

Christine looked hurt. She stopped in her tracks. "You're about as sweet as they get, aren't you?"

"Politeness is not one of my endearing characteristics. Honesty is."

"As if."

"What does that mean?"

"No one is honest. Everyone is out for themselves and will say whatever they can think to say that will get them what they want."

"I don't want anything."

She laughed, which really freaked me out. Because it changed her entire face, her whole being. I mean, she really looked pretty instead of hard. But it vanished quickly like the sun cracking through the heavy clouds of a dark day—a quick tease and then a vanishing act that left you feeling even worse than before. "Oh, you want something, Dreamboy. We all want something, even when we don't know what it is." Then she scrunched up her nose. I think she was sucking back snot. "You want a beer?"

"You got beer?"

"I got a couple of cans left. Just don't go asking me a bunch of personal questions."

"Hey, I thought you wanted to tell me your life story. Besides, why should I care?"

"That's better. What did you say your name was, Dreamboy?"

For a second, I thought of making something up. Of lying to her. I wasn't really sure I wanted her to know I was from the school for rich kids with problems. "Carson," I said.

"What kind of freaking name is that?"

"Blame my parents," I said. We had stopped by the most beat-up looking mobile home on Sneezy Lane. The screen in the door had been kicked out. Christine yanked hard to get it to open. "Watch the step."

"What step?" It had rusted and fallen off a long time ago. It was a big leg up to enter this place. Inside, it looked like someone had recently sacked the room. My eyes tried to adjust to the light. All the curtains were closed. The smell was mildew and something toxic, Raid maybe. Something sprayed to kill bugs. "Are you always this neat or were you expecting company?"

She put her hand on her hip in a kind of nasty, kind of sexy way. "You want that beer or not?"

"Sure."

She found a screwdriver and stuck it in a slot in the refrigerator door where the handle had broken off. It opened with a satisfying click and she looked very alien indeed in the cold misty light that emanated from within. She brought out two tall cans and handed me one. "It's eight percent," she said. "Go easy."

"Eight percent?"

"Alcohol, Dreamboy. It's like beer with a lot of alcohol in it."

"Oh." I took a sip and it didn't taste like any beer I'd ever tasted. Kind of sweet and, oh yeah, lots of kick to it.

"It's German, I think. Guy down the road gave it to me, thinking he could get me drunk and . . . well, you know. But it didn't work. And then his wife figured out he was here, came over and tore the place apart. She hauled him outside and actually hit him on the head with a shovel."

"Jesus."

"You think that's bad, you should see what goes on up on Dopey Drive."

I took another sip of the high-end beer and wondered what kind of B movie I'd walked into. Don't know if it was the beer or the girl or sitting in the middle of all the trailer trash that was getting to me but I suddenly felt—how can I say this?—I felt not so bad.

"So how do you like my life so far?" she asked. She scrunched up her nose again and looked at the water-stained ceiling.

"It's not so bad."

"Try living it from the inside."

I was looking at her arms again, the scars. She noticed and got up and went into what must have been a bedroom. She came back with a big, dirty sweatshirt on.

"Your parents around?" I knew I was in no-man's-land here, wondered if a father or mother would come home, see me sitting with their daughter drinking beer. I was wondering what it felt like to be hit flat-face with a shovel or some other farm implement.

"My father's long gone. My mom . . . haven't seen her in . . . hmm . . . maybe a month. New boyfriend plays in a band.

Lots of road time. I've got to cover her tracks sometimes. But that's enough of that." She slugged back some German beer. "People don't really call you Carson, do they?"

"Yeah. That's my name."

"But it sounds like some guy who hosts a game show or bakes cookies or something. You don't bake cookies, do you?"

"Give me a break."

A hint of a smile again, a small ribbon of sunlight. "Somewhere along the way you must have had a nickname. Give."

No one at FOA had ever gotten it out of me. It was from childhood, and, sad to say, it was even of my own invention. "Nosrac," I told her.

"Nosrac? No way."

Already the regret. I think my face was getting red. "Carson spelled backwards. I saw it in a mirror. I thought there could be this other me. I was freaking ten years old, for God's sake. I was watching a lot of bad science fiction movies. I was hoping to invent the alternate me."

"Nosrac," she repeated. "So did you succeed at the alternate you?"

"No. Failed miserably. Every morning I'd wake up and it was still me. It sucked. I wanted to be somewhere else, somebody else."

"Can I call you Nosrac?" She was giggling now.

"No," I insisted. "If you do, I'll call you Enitsirhc."

I think she was going to laugh out loud. I think she got it and thought it was funny but she swallowed the laugh. She became serious again. "You go to that school, don't you?"

"Yeah. And I know what everyone in this town thinks about us."

"Rich and spoiled and as screwed-up as they come."

"Pretty much covers it," I said. "And there's no way out."

"What do you mean?"

"I mean . . . about what you said. We *are* who we are. And it's not like we're going to change or be cured or anything like that. Once they put us out on the street we have to take our baggage with us. What about you? You go to Hooterville High?"

"I'll show up for a class once in a while. But it's not like they're going to graduate me or anything. My big goal in life is to stay a couple of steps ahead of the social workers so they don't lock me into a group home. But once I hit seventeen, I'm out of here."

A car without a muffler went by right then and it sounded like it was right in the room with us. "Where would you go?" I asked.

She fell back into her own darkness just then and sipped the beer. "That's the funny part. I'm not sure there is anywhere *to* go."

Chapter Five

I got a little buzz on from the beer. It was pretty powerful stuff but she had warned me about the alcohol content.

"You can hang out here for a while if you want," Christine said. She was back to looking pretty unhappy. Unhappy. Unhealthy. Unloved. Un-everything. Just put "un" in front of any word you could think of and it would be her.

The trouble with a good daytime beer buzz is that when it starts to fade you feel drained and more bummed out than ever. I was looking for the exit but didn't want to hurt her feelings. That part was freaking me out inside my head. Why did I give a flying fart about her feelings?

"Look, I have to get back to the school. Thanks for the beer."

She looked glum and sucked back some air. "What are you afraid of?"

That made me defensive. "I'm not afraid of anything."

She slugged back the last of her beer. "You think I'm trying to get you drunk and then I'll rip your clothes off?"

I gave her my best as-if look. I should have known better

than to let this girl mess around with my head. "Listen, it's been a real slice here this afternoon but, like, I was cutting school and I should get back before anyone makes too big a deal out of it."

"What can they do? Kick you out?"

Well, as you may recall, the truth was that no one ever gets kicked out of FOA. We were the last stop before the door opened and we were emptied like so much rich white trash back onto the streets of the real world. And none of us was all that anxious for that event. I shook my head. "Can you read what it says on my forehead?"

She looked at me hard, didn't get it.

"Can't read the big block letters: BORN TO FAIL?"

"Look who's feeling sorry for himself."

I looked around at my surroundings for a split second and got the point but still felt defensive. "I'm a big fat disappointment to my parents."

"At least you have parents." She was sucking on her lip now. I saw that sad and hurt but almost pretty face that I had noticed before. I knew what she was doing. She wanted me to feel sorry for her. I could see this was her routine. I wondered what she wanted from me after that. I decided to stick with my plan: cut my losses here and get back, tell Cromwell that the cut classes, the beer were temporary insanity.

"You gonna be okay?" I tried to sound sincere but I was really just looking for the door.

"Maybe I'll go find that guy down the street and see if he has another beer to spare."

"The guy who got hit in the face with the shovel?"

"Maybe he won't remember that part."

"Anyway, see ya."

• • •

She didn't say goodbye. As I opened up the aluminum door and stepped out, I nearly fell on my face—I'd forgotten about the missing metal step. I decided to put the afternoon out of my mind. The last thing I needed was a girl like this in my life. The last thing I needed was anyone. I walked purposefully and quickly down from the trailer park and into town. *Stay focused, Carson. Keep your wits about you. Look out for number one and you might survive for a few more years on this despicable, screwed-up planet.*

• • •

Harborville was a green and leafy place at this time of year. As I walked towards the school, the lawns became more immaculate, the trees were larger, and the flowers more abundant in the yards. The cars were more expensive, the dogs smaller, and the sidewalks improved. I couldn't help thinking that it was all a cover-up. Inside those houses were people with families as injured as Christine's in their own ways. If you had money, you could make things look better than they really were. It seemed that every kid in my school had a good reason to be there. Most had not been beaten or abused by their parents, but something almost as bad had happened to them. Many had been simply set aside, ignored, while their parents got on with their busy, important lives.

Sometimes I reckoned that I was the only kid at FOA who deserved to be there. It wasn't my parents who had failed me. It was me. I had screwed up my own life every opportunity I could get despite my parents' best efforts. Look at my brother, Ben. Ben was okay. Ben was on cruise control, having a good time of it in high school back where I came from. I was the family screwup and I had earned my reputation well.

• • •

Our Harborville neighbors had complained loud and often about Farnsworth and how it looked. The leaves piled up on the lawn, the broken tree branches, the rusty wrought iron fence, the blown trash accumulating in said fence, the unpainted old house itself, the slate shingles that would periodically slide off the roof one by one. It had once been a fine building, well-maintained by a capitalist icon. Now it was a run-down palace of sorts, a faded and falling-down mansion that was also my home.

I walked in and realized that the whole school—all thirty-five students, for this was an elite academy of rich-ass losers—were gathered in the library where Dr. Cromwell was giving one of his famous lectures. But I could tell from the tone it wasn't a pep talk this time. I crept in and leaned against the back wall next to Fin, as if I'd been there all along. No one seemed to notice except Mr. Dodd who lifted his eyebrows knowingly. The other teachers were whispering conspiratorially with each other as I'd seen them do before while drinking coffee in the school kitchen.

"So, you see, what we have here is a kind of fiscal crisis. I've notified your parents but few have come forward. Your parents are very busy people, I understand, but we've hit a point where we need their financial commitment if we want to put lunch on the table for you tomorrow."

Code-X was the first to interrupt. "Dr. Cromwell, how come you always have to put these things so politely? What I hear you saying is that some of our parents are not paying their bills. They send us here, leave you to take care of us, and then fly off to Vegas or Australia."

The famous Cromwell hand was held out, palm forward in front of him. "I'm not saying your parents are negligent."

Well, the truth was he was saying that many of the parents *were* negligent. It was an old story around Farnsworth and explained why the place was such a dump. The big cars drove up the cracked and weedy driveway in September, the luggage (along with son or daughter) were deposited on the front steps, and the big cars drove off down the street. And not every student was necessarily invited to come back home for Christmas. Code-X was a case in point. He took Cromwell to task, as he often did. "My father is like a real sphincter muscle when it comes to money, I know that. No one gets cash out of him until he gets the third letter from the lawyer. He says that's the only way to stay in business." Ryan's father was in the importing business. He imported "novelty items" for sex shops across North America and, according to Ryan, he was quite successful.

Cromwell mustered up a paternal smile. "I'm hoping that lawyers are not the answer. When lawyers are involved, things only get worse."

This prompted Giselle to pipe up, "My father's a lawyer."

"So is mine," added Mary.

This made Cromwell clear his throat with great ambition and add, "I didn't mean that to come out the wrong way."

Strangely, most of us rather liked old crazy Doc Cromwell. It was obvious to most of us that he was very intelligent but most probably insane. Why would anyone in his right mind have created this place? Or bother to spend his life dedicated to an academy of teenagers whose parents didn't even want them around?

Of the dregs of society, there are poor dregs and rich dregs. We were the rich dregs. But then, why did I even care what he did with his life? And why should I care about his problems? But in truth, I think, I did care. And that felt truly weird.

"So you want us to call up our parents and beg them to pay up or you'll boot us out?" Mary asked now with a kind of breathless shock in her voice.

The hand again. "No, Mary. All I'm asking is that you remind them of their financial responsibility in the most polite and respectful manner." You could tell this was a real struggle for Doc and I felt bad for him. He was such a sucker. It must have been the beer speaking when I blurted out, "I'll call home this afternoon."

Cromwell blinked and tried to focus on me in the back of the small crowd. I was now leaning against the musty, faded drapes. "Carson, that's much appreciated but, ahem, your tuition, room, and board is already paid in full."

I nodded silently. I probably should have known this. My parents were always, always by-the-book. They were always, I knew, good parents. Look at the way Ben turned out. Normal as you could get. And they tried with me. They really did.

Code-X spoke again. "Dr. C., I feel your pain, man. And

I want to personally apologize for having a genuine asshole for a father. Some of us are not as lucky as Carson over there. Squeezing money out of my old man—I mean, did you ever try to, well, get blood from a stone? What would you think about an alternative fund-raising endeavor? With a little up-front capital, possibly a loan from Carson's responsible mommy and daddy, we could raise enough cash to further all our education in a most comfortable manner."

Dr. Cromwell knew where this was headed. Code-X, rarely in touch with much of anything to do with the real world, talked freely about his plans to hire a private plane and fly to Colombia and load it with cocaine. He claimed to have contacts down there in the jungle and that the whole enterprise was "easy." His goal in life was to be an "entrepreneur in recreational drugs." The students were already laughing. They too saw where this was going. Code-X was as predictable as you got. He really believed that a couple of big dope deals would set him up for life and he'd live happily ever after. Now, in a fit of compassion for Cromwell and a seasoning of generosity, here he was sharing his grand ambition with us in order to bail out the school.

Cromwell asked for order. "I am truly embarrassed to be bringing any of this up with you but I don't know what else to do. I'll hand out sheets with the amounts owing and ask you to call home tonight. Please be respectful to your folks. They want what is best for you and I expect that this is just an oversight."

That was it. Papers were handed out. Some kids were laughing. But for others, I saw the look in their eyes. The look was fear. Mary looked pale and Giselle seemed nervous. Code-X seemed as casual as ever. Maybe he already knew deep down he was going to set himself up to spend the rest of the days of his life in a federal prison anyway, so why bother worrying about anything.

But there was a nervous tension in the air. Furtive eyes. Either my classmates were afraid to confront their parents about this or they had a genuine fear that this place might close down and we'd all have to go back to our homes.

I was still dwelling on the stupid irony. Everyone came from parents who had money, lots of money. Money to burn. And so many of those same parents were delinquent in paying for their sons' and daughters' living expenses and education. This issue had been raised before but never like this. Cromwell was in trouble. FOA was in trouble.

"Carson, you have a minute?" Cromwell asked as the room emptied.

I popped a piece of gum into my mouth. "Sure."

Chapter Six

The French doors to the library were closed and silence descended. Dr. Cromwell asked me to have a seat. He could tell I'd been drinking but chose not to say anything about it. "I hear that you are studying the Punic Wars in history," he said matter-of-factly. "Ever read the first-person accounts of the events as set down by a writer named Appian?"

"Can't say that I have." I could fathom why he wanted to talk about ancient warfare between Rome and Carthage. He knew that war was on my ultra-short list of academic interests. "Almost a hundred years of war," I said. "You got to wake up and take notice of that," I said. "Thousands dead. A whole city eventually burned down to the desert. Human ambition at its best."

Cromwell cringed at the word "best."

"You probably liked the part about Hannibal," he said.

"A minor setback for the Romans. All it took was time and money and inevitably Carthage would fall."

"Inevitably? Really? What do you think this long on-again, off-again war was really about?"

"Greed, power, lust for control, and domination."

"Aren't you glad we don't live in those times?" Cromwell said it with a straight face but I knew he was working me. He wasn't that naive.

"To the winner go the spoils. Then or now. Pretty much the same deal. History repeats itself because human nature stays the same."

"Not all of us believe that."

"You've been trying to save the world since you were what, eleven?" I said.

"Ten actually."

"How's it coming?"

"It's an uphill struggle. Look at this mess I'm in now."

The odd thing about Dr. Cromwell's madness was that he wielded his authority so lightly at times. Oh, he could burn you down with a stare if he wanted to. He could appear fiery and even demonic and make you slink off to your room. But usually he tried this calm and reasoned approach and made himself seem downright vulnerable. It worked on the kids, but it must not have worked on their parents with their tight financial sphincter muscles.

It was as if Cromwell was looking for my advice, and I knew this was one of his famous shrink tactics for getting at something within me. I decided to return to the Punic Wars. "Well, Dr. C., remember what Hannibal did in the second Punic war? Thirty thousand troops and a long-ass haul over the Alps to get at the Romans. And using elephants—that would have to have come as a shock to the Romans, seeing elephants coming down from the mountains."

"A brilliant strategist, Hannibal. Maybe if we had a few

elephants, I could save the school."

"That and 30,000 troops," I reminded him. "But in the end, the Romans still got revenge, right? They whipped the Carthaginians. I forget what happened to Hannibal, himself."

"You don't want to know."

"I'm always up for the truth, Doc, you know me. Even if it hurts," I said.

"He ended up in Syria, still fighting the Romans, but losing. So he poisoned himself."

"Took the easy way out," I heard myself saying, suddenly feeling sorry for Hannibal, the innovative leader who crossed mountains with elephants, and died as a sorry loser like the rest of us.

Cromwell clasped his dramatic hands in front of him, a predictor of a shift in the discussion about to occur. "Two things on my mind that I wanted to talk to you about."

"Can't we just stick to death and destruction?"

"It would be fun but there are other pressing matters. The first one is your parents."

"What about my parents?" I didn't like the sudden shift and felt a curious panic in the back of my brain.

He saw my look. "Nothing like that. They're coming down here. Tomorrow. They offered to help me with my little campaign here to bring the school back to some kind of solvency."

"Always the do-gooders," I said. "Did they ask about me?"

"Of course. They wanted to know how you were doing. I told them you were doing fine."

"You lied then."

"Well, I chose not to tell them you were failing math and I didn't say anything about the content of your English paper, if that is what you mean."

"Why not?"

"I don't know, okay?" he said and then sighed. "So cut me some slack on that."

"Whatever."

"So after we meet in the afternoon, they want to take you out to dinner."

"With Ben?"

"No, I think your brother has a wrestling match or something."

"We wrestled when we were kids. He was younger and yet he always won—smarter, stronger, more desire to win. Now, he'll probably make a career out of it or at least get a scholarship to university."

"About your parents . . . they worry about you."

"Do they ever ask why you haven't figured me out yet?"

"No. They only want what's best for you."

"So it's going to be the whole guilt trip again." I clammed up after that. The old, sad tale was a simple one. My parents were good people. They did all the right things and I should have grown up to be a perfect son. But I messed that up good, over and over. FOA was a kind of end-of-the-line institution and we all knew it. Doc most of all. And he knew if he shut down the crumbling mansion, we'd be a sorry lot of damaged humans in a sorry, sorry world.

"Just go out to dinner with them and give them a chance."

He almost sounded like he was begging me to do it for his sake.

"No problem."

He got up to go. "Oh, and keep an eye on Griffin. I think he might be going through a hard time. *Ciao.*"

• • •

Cromwell had never once mentioned the beer on my breath. And I was having a bit of a hard time trying to figure out precisely what this little talk was really aimed at. I always felt that way after Dr. Crum had one of his chats with me and I wondered if the other kids felt the same way.

My room had that familiar aroma of stale farts and dirty socks, signature Griffin olfactory traits. Fin was, predictably, on the Internet, in a chat room discussing God knows what with who knows who. "Where ya been, man?" he asked.

"I needed some air," I said. "Walked around downtown and met a girl."

"You met a girl?" He turned away from his video screen and looked at me.

"Well, it wasn't like that. She was just there down by the water. We had a couple of beers. In the end it kind of sucked. She was pretty messed up."

"Wow." Fin's reaction was genuine. He didn't have that much direct contact with girls, even though half of the student body were of that persuasion. Fin had a grasp of nuclear physics equal to that of a third-year university physics major. He was a kind of world-class expert on the history of the twentieth-century arms race. He actually got As in all of his subjects and did all the required and suggested readings and all of the homework. Yet he didn't have a clue about anything else.

I remember what Cromwell had said to me at the end of our little discussion. It suddenly occurred to me that this was what it might have been all about—not about me at all, but Fin.

I flopped down on my bed and lay there looking at the ceiling. "Anything new with you, Fin?" Now I would play the shrink and see what there was to learn about my baffled, lost but brilliant roommate.

"Same old, same old," he said, back to clicking away at the keyboard, chatting with whoever he was chatting with.

"Really?"

"Well, I had an e-mail from my dad," he added, his voice dropping in volume to barely audible. His fingers stopped tapping keys.

"That was a rare treat," I said, trying to mask the sarcasm. Fin's father had made a fortune as an aeronautical engineer. He had started his own corporation and come up with a guidance system for military missiles that was bought up by nearly a dozen countries. The bizarre part of it was that it was based on something to do with pigeons and their ability to fly in perfect balance in daylight or in the dark.

"You know what he said?" Fin asked, now actually turning my way.

"What?" I was still staring at the ceiling.

"He said he was going to Singapore for a while."

"Singapore?"

"You know, near Indonesia."

"I know where Singapore is. So?"

"So he said he might stay there for some time."

"Did he say why?"

"Something to do with a woman he met over the Internet."

"Give me a break."

"It's what he said. He thinks he's in love."

"Isn't he kind of old for that? What about your mother?"

"He didn't mention anything about her."

"Cromwell will never get him to pay up now."

"Yeah."

I wasn't much good at this sympathy thing. I tried to imagine what Cromwell would want me to say but all I could come up with was, "So how do you feel?"

"I don't know," Fin said.

A tangible and awkward silence ensued. The kind you could slice up with a carving knife and serve up for the most uncomfortable family meal imaginable.

"Hey," Fin said, "what did Cromwell want to see you about? You get into trouble or something? Was it the girl?"

"No, he just wanted to talk about the Punic Wars."

"Like in history class?"

"Yeah. Hey, check this out." I walked over to his computer and, ignoring the fact that he didn't want me to touch anything, I clicked on Google and typed in "Appian" and "Punic Wars." I found what I was looking for.

I flipped through a couple of screens and lucked onto a passage about what Carthage looked like after the Romans had ruined the African city. I read to Fin out loud: "The Roman troops were told to clean up the city. They pushed the dead and some still living into pits and, using axes and crowbars, pushed them like stones or blocks of wood until bodies filled the gullies. Some, tossed in head down with their legs sticking out of the ground, writhed for some time after they were buried. Some were left with heads protruding. Their faces and skulls were trampled by galloping horses."

Fin looked at me and blinked.

"Wow," Fin said. And then he swallowed hard and looked at me like I had just revealed some amazing discovery.

Chapter Seven

I was one of those unfortunate sons who did not have perfectly legitimate reasons for hating his parents. If your father manufactured napalm or if your mother ran a fashion corporation that made its millions from exploiting child labor in Southeast Asia, a boy could feel self-righteous with indignation and rage against his parents.

But, sadly, that was not my case. My parents had done their level best to be good to me and I had still turned out badly. In the nature versus nurture argument about what shapes a child—heredity or environment—I most likely was some product of (or freak of) nature. Somewhere in our family tree must have been an ancestor who had been a supreme screw-up, someone who harbored ill will against the world and stored it up in his genetic code secure enough to pass it down to a progeny in the distant future.

That progeny being myself, yours truly, Carson Sullivan.

But about my parents.

My father, early in his career and fresh out of university, decided that the world needed saving from pollution, global warming, and corporate greed, so he went into the "alternate energy" business. He took his engineering degree and put it to good use developing wind and solar energy. His small company grew slowly at first but every time the price of a barrel of oil lifted, so did interest in my father's work. He planted wind turbines, small and large, on pillars and posts. He strapped solar collectors onto the roofs of rich men's houses. He came home one day with an electric car, for God's sakes, the first one anyone in our neighborhood had ever seen up close. He showed TV, radio, and newspaper alike that all he had to do was plug it into the power source at home, tapping into electricity produced by our own backyard wind generator and then drive his vehicle happily and silently on his way.

My father was nearly ego-less. He did not thrive on the glory of being an earth-saving energy pioneer. Instead, he would offer to take his sons, me and Ben, hiking or swimming or mountain biking. The trouble was I usually didn't want to go. I was angry a lot while I was growing up. I was angry at him because there was something wrong—wrong with the world and wrong with me. And I didn't know what to do about it but seethe.

My mother, through my youth, was one of that dying breed of women once known as housewives. While Dad was out harnessing the wind and tapping sunlight for heat and otherwise quietly driving a silent, non-polluting car, Mom stayed at home raising her boys. She had read a virtual library on raising children to be happy, fun-loving, non-violent, productive humans. She took it all to heart and I should have turned out to be a saint. Ben, two years my junior, turned out to be smart, athletic, popular, and at home in the world. I stumbled in the world as often as I stood, however. I didn't seem to have the knack for social skills even at an early age. They say I stole from my classmates even in grade one, cheated on spelling tests as soon as they appeared on my youthful curriculum, said cruel and even obscene things to my teachers, and was not reputed to be anything but rude and inconsiderate to my classmates.

After that I got worse.

Mom dutifully drove me in the family electric car to counsellors and shrinks, and read more books. At one point, she was convinced that a change in diet would mend my ways. Hence we all became vegetarians, an initiative, my dad said, that was "long overdue."

Ben complained but went along with the diet that turned out to trim him down so that he ended up being a champion wrestler in his weight class. While wrestling did not at first seem to fit into the earth-saving, pacifist vegetarian lifestyle, there was parental agreement that it was a healthy outlet for aggression and they even tried to steer me onto the wrestling mat. I was, as it turned out, reluctant to wrestle according to the rulebook and after I punched Brad Lecker, I was "let go" from the wrestling team.

While Ben was growing up to become a much-applauded play-it-by-the-rules regional wrestling champ and I was continually stumbling off the path of kindness into the dark jungle of my own malevolence, my mom washed our clothes, cooked complex exotic and sometimes inedible meals that I often referred to as "rabbit food," and took up charitable work. Wielding phone and notebook, she persuaded local politicians to abolish pesticides, solicited money for women's centres in Sri Lanka, lobbied drug companies to donate free drugs to AIDS victims in Africa, mounted publicity campaigns to save leatherback turtles in Central America, and, cell phone jammed between ear and shoulder, baked cookies to sell for the wrestling team's upcoming trip to the national competition.

As the years rolled by and my earth-saving parents began to realize that I was not turning out as planned, they eased up on their campaign to mold me into a model citizen. "Carson is going to be Carson," I heard my father say to my mother as they sat on the front porch one sweltering summer evening. "He's going to turn out fine," my mother said, a perpetual optimist despite the ever-present evidence of myself.

• • •

I looked out the window at 4:30 and saw my father driving his modest little electric car in through the sagging metal gates of the Farnsworth estate. He parked carefully between the white lines of the visitor's parking space and he and my mother entered the building. Seeing them below my window filled me with a cocktail of emotions: shame, regret, sorrow, confusion. Somewhere in there I want to say there was love, but that emotion seemed unable to wrestle against the conspiracy of the others that pinned it to the mat.

• • •

My dad was looking older—hair thinner, wrinkles around the eyes. He hugged me first and then my mom held me to her tightly. She seemed much the same as always. She sniffled as she hugged me and I understood what that was about. "We miss you," she whispered, although I knew deep down that life at home was easier for them all when I was not around. Brother Gloom, Ben called me sometimes.

When my dad said hi to Fin, he received in return a full two-syllable reply from my roommate and then the Finster returned to his chat room and his anonymous friends around the planet who were trying to locate renegade plutonium.

"How's school?" my mom asked me.

"So far so good," I said, revealing nothing.

"Are you getting enough to eat?" my dad asked. "Do they give you enough fresh fruit and vegetables?"

"The food is great," I said. Mrs. Chin fed us what she knew we would eat, not necessarily what was good for us and that's what we all liked about her. My father and mother thought that all world problems could be fixed if everyone ate like them—healthy and boring. It was a naive theory that couldn't stand up to cheeseburgers and french fries.

My mother had just let go of me when she suddenly reached towards me and gave me a second hug. She tried to pretend that she wasn't weepy but I knew she had a hard time each time they saw me.

Awkward conversation ensued concerning wind turbine design, education, roughage, sweat shops, ozone depletion, and Ben's wrestling matches. And then they went downstairs to meet with Dr. Cromwell to help him with his "fiscal situation." Dinner would come later. I was so not looking forward to that.

• • •

I had forgotten how quiet the electric car was. With no radio or CD player on, the silence of driving with my parents was even more disconcerting than the silence of driving in a conventional car. "We'll be pretty close to pushing the limit on driving range by the time we get home this evening," my dad said, explaining why he was driving so slowly. "But I'm sure we're okay."

My mother nodded reassuringly. She trusted my father and his decisions. The issue was driving range: how far you could go in an electric before the battery needed recharging. It required a special plug-in, like the one he had at home. You couldn't just run an extension cord out of any place and recharge.

"I like to think that we're not really using electricity at all," my mother said. "It's the wind that powers the car."

Leave it to Mom to make driving a stupid car sound poetic. What she meant was that the juice that kept us moving was stored voltage that had, only yesterday, been generated in our backyard by twin blades of the wind generator.

We slid silently into a parking place on the street in front of Alfredo's, Harborville's only truly expensive restaurant. God, how I hated expensive restaurants and the inevitable discussions about food—what to eat, what not to eat. And I knew if I ordered red meat, I'd get a lecture. Why bother?

When I got out of the car I saw her. She was walking down the street panhandling from the people walking past her. "Got any change? Can you spare something, please?"

Before I could hurry my parents into Alfredo's she had walked up to us. "I'm really hoping you can help me out," she said to my mother who was ahead of me. Christine hadn't noticed me and I think that, maybe if I had turned my back to her, she wouldn't, and then she'd be on her way. But it was too late.

My mother was opening her purse. Christine noticed me. "Carson," she said.

"Hey," I said back.

My mom stopped fishing in her purse. My dad had a curious look on his face.

Christine's long, uncombed hair hung down over her face. She had on a flannel shirt tucked into dirty jeans, and she was wearing beat-up sandals. She seemed perfectly comfortable begging from strangers but now that she saw me I saw something else in her face, in her eyes. She was suddenly nervous and uncertain.

"These are my parents," I said sheepishly. My dad nodded and looked at the sidewalk. My mom stared into her purse and then back at the street girl.

"And this is Christine," I said awkwardly.

Chapter Eight

I wanted to punch the waiter. I really did. I have a ninety-five percent scumbag rating for waiters. That is, ninety-five percent of the waiters I've ever encountered are loathsome. Five percent are tolerable. The jury is out about waitresses. Some try to be nice. Some have that bored, dead-in-the-eye look, some can be nasty and pushy. But for waiters, that's a different story. It's like they went to some class where they were told, "Be nice to the parents. They have the money. They will maybe leave you a good tip. Suck up to the ladies. Indulge the men their sodden humor. But when you see the kid, make him feel like he is dirty underwear."

That's what I felt like in Alfredo's. Dirty underwear. Having Christine at the table with us compounded the problem. I was wishing we were just at McDonald's having a quick and greasy one. But that would have never happened in my family. Red meat and decimated Amazon rainforests. Trans fats, palm oil fries, ozone-depleting plates, cups, and utensils. That would have been my idea of heaven compared to this.

Christine did not turn down the offer of a free meal at

Alfredo's. As we were seated by the vile maître d', Christine admitted, "I've never been inside here before. It's really nice." I kept hoping she'd keep the sleeves of her shirt rolled down. It was warm in here. Too warm. And I detected a faint hint of beer on her breath. My mom had scrunched up her nose. She must have noticed it too. I was wishing I had been free to spend the evening back in my academy room with some thumbscrews maybe or a nice warm cup of hemlock.

My parents had an amazing cool about them. They saw how the maître d', a thin man with a dark jacket who seemed to have stepped out of a horror movie, looked at Christine. The waiter gave her the same look. She pretended not to notice. Neither of my parents asked her about why she was begging for change on the street. My mother had never given her the five she was reaching for. I know it was a five, because that is what my mom gave to panhandlers. Not a quarter, not a dollar or two. A fiver. She was the sort who wanted to help.

Christine brushed her hair out of her eyes so that we could all see the several hooped piercings in her left eyebrow and the darkness beneath those eyes that seemed so sad, so hurt. I was nervous as anything sitting there with her and my parents, expecting Christine to say something really embarrassing. I really wished that she had turned down the invitation when invited. She should have seen that this was going to be awful. She could have done me this favor and let me suffer with my parents on my own. But the truth was that she was probably hungry.

"Are you hungry?" my father asked her.

"I haven't eaten yet today," she said. Then she corrected herself. "That's not really true. I had some toast this morning."

Toast. Jesus.

"Order whatever you like," my mom said.

I wanted to wade in here and point out the location of the explosives in this minefield. "My parents are, ahem . . ."

But she interrupted me. She pointed to something on the overly large, laminated multi-age menu. "I'm going to go for the steak. Is that okay?"

In my mother's imagination, Amazon basin jungles were burning to give way to pasture land. A cow was being fed raw chemicals and hormones and eventually killed by a teenage boy with an electric stun-hammer to the cow brain. Blood was dripping into gutters and raw meat hanging from rafters as the flies buzzed. She cleared her throat. "That would be lovely," she said.

"I'll have the same," I said. "Medium rare." It'd been a long time.

The despicable waiter came and my mother ordered her quiche, my father (still a believer that a vegetarian could eat seafood) ordered the salmon and, on our behalf, he swallowed his pride and ordered up two slabs of meat for the youth at the table.

"Wine with that?" asked our humble servant.

Christine looked my way, hopeful. I shook my head no.

"Not tonight, thanks," my dad said. "Maybe a little Perrier all around."

Nothing like a little fizzy French water to wash down prime sirloin. I thought about tripping the waiter. I wanted to get my mind off the current social dilemma and wondered if I could get away with it. I would work the angles but there was no easy way to make it happen without being noticed. It was one of the greater disappointments of the evening.

"How long have you and Carson been . . . um . . . friends?" my mom asked Christine.

"Not long," she answered. "We met at the harbor. He likes staring into the water and so do I."

My father gave me that curious look again. "I'm hoping to become a marine biologist," I said. It was a bold-faced lie of course. Christine giggled a little and I was afraid she was going to say something really stupid but instead she looked at me and she smiled. And something inside of me broke. Or melted. Or something. I don't know what it was and it scared me a little. And it made me feel crazy. It made me feel—sorry, this is hard to explain—funny. Light-headed. Almost nauseous.

No. It made me feel, well . . . good.

"You go to school here in town?" Pretty astute of my mom to assume that a girl begging for quarters on the street wasn't from the rich-ass school up the hill.

"I do. I live at home."

"Oh," Dad said, "and what does your father do?" He should have known better.

I was back into the trip-the-waiter fantasy mode. The Perrier was arriving and I missed my chance. I looked around at the paintings on the walls, all very Italian, very Renaissance, very fake. I kept wishing for the chandelier to fall from the ceiling or for an earthquake but could not conjure the code. Christine smiled at the question, decided not to get into it. "He's not around much," was all she said. "What do you do?" she asked. I was pretty freaked out to see how comfortable she had suddenly become with my parents.

"Do you want the short version or the long?"

"Just give her the Coles notes on it, Dad. Not the whole career."

Even the Coles notes version was a little windy but that and some friendly comments from my mother took us up to the main course. I watched my mother looking at Christine as her knife cut into the dead cow meat. She looked on in a kind of muffled horror as the fork was lifted to the mouth and then my mom looked down at her pale parsley-bedecked quiche. She couldn't seem to muster the will to eat but moved the three string beans on her plate around with her knife as if rearranging furniture in a living room.

I ate my own meal with trepidation. I expected any minute something would go wrong. I don't know why I even cared but I did. I realized that I actually wanted my parents to like Christine.

And they did, I think, at least a little. They didn't lecture her at least or say anything stupid.

"Marine biology?" my dad suddenly asked me out of the blue.

"Hey, the planet's mostly covered with water, right?" I said.

"There's a heck of a lot we don't yet understand about the seas or the living things in them."

"That's what I was thinking, precisely," I said.

I think my parents understood I wasn't really serious.

But I could see that I had shocked them. What had I done? I wondered, sipping my French water and looking up at Christine. She was smiling at me. Gravity was suspended on planet earth for a quick flash of time.

And then it occurred to me. I had just exhibited a sense of humor. I cleared my throat. "Plankton," I said rather loudly.

My parents stopped eating and looked at me.

"I want to study plankton. Start at the bottom and work my way up."

Chapter Nine

My parents seemed strangely satisfied with the evening. Despite my advice, they gave a sizeable tip to the waiter. I caught the creep giving Christine a dirty look from across the room while we were eating. My plan was to phone the town health inspector in the morning and report that I had seen this guy drooling or spitting or dripping snot into somebody's soup and then serving it. The plan gave me my own brand of satisfaction even if I didn't act upon it.

Christine had refused a ride home from my parents, saying she only lived up the street. We were all spared a trip down Sneezy Lane. On the way back to Farnsworth, my father was beginning to worry if the electrical charge on the car would get them home. He hadn't driven it this far from home before and it was a bit of a test. "I figure we have a margin of error of maybe ten minutes. I'll have to drive moderately, though, even at that."

"Your father knows what he's doing," my mom said reassuringly.

"Everyone thinks that if the petroleum runs out, it will

be the end of the world as we know it," my dad said. "But it will be the beginning of a much better world, believe me."

I envisioned a world of backyard wind generators and solar heated homes. Shiny, happy people, quiet cars, no pollution, no wars over oil fields, nobody freezing or starving. It was a pipe dream. It was part of an optimistic vision that my father carried around in his head day after day.

And that world would never happen.

In my gut I knew that things would only get worse.

My mom gave me a hug when they dropped me off at the school. "You'll have to tell us more about Christine, sometime," she said.

"I will," I lied.

Dr. Cromwell was in the hallway vacuuming when I walked in. He took me completely by surprise.

"Dr. C.?"

He flicked off the noisy machine.

"Just tidying up," he said.

"Yeah, but why you? Why now?"

"The caretaker quit, I'm afraid. Jason was a good worker but he just wasn't sure this job would be around all that much longer. He found work elsewhere. So here I am. Want to help?"

"No."

"I find it . . . refreshing. Setting the world right. Order. Cleanliness. All that. I don't mind it a bit, really."

Although I often found Cromwell's attitude a bit too positive for my liking, seeing him vacuuming dust from the hallway made me think that this was just the tip of the iceberg. Whenever I felt the slightest little buzz of something good—let's call it optimism for the future—the dark clouds came roaring in out of the north with a cold harsh wind and I felt iciness in my chest.

The end of the world as we know it.

I envisioned my father's car with the dead battery stalled on the highway ten miles from home. The closing of Farnsworth Academy. My inevitable induction into the so-called real world beyond seventeen. And, as I clomped up the stairway, one hand on the great oak banister that wobbled under the touch, I saw how crazy it would be to involve myself with someone as messed-up as Christine. Hey, she got a free meal out of my old man and she got through the evening without saying anything really stupid. Let's call that a successful night and leave it at that.

In my room, I fell asleep to the sound of Cromwell down below, vacuuming the old library, the sound of Cromwell trying to "set the world right" while the walls were crumbling around him, while slate tiles were sliding from the roof and crashing into the weedy flowerbeds.

Fin snored in his sleep and, oddly enough, it never bothered me. I fell asleep to his rhythmic hoarse breathing, the vacuuming downstairs, and the rising wind outside that seeped in through the leaky windows. I now remembered a childhood fantasy that had stayed with me for years when I was a kid. It went like this:

One night, with everything perfectly normal, you go to bed after arguing with your brother and watching TV shows that he wants to watch. Something happens in the night and by morning everything has disappeared. Everything, including you. And it is as if nothing . . . nothing ever existed. You, your family, your house, your neighborhood. Everything and everybody gone without a trace.

I found that little trip of the imagination very comforting and had put myself to sleep thinking about it many times before. The great disappointment was always waking up in the morning and realizing it was just a dream. The world would still be there. And so was I.

• • •

The next few days of school went as normally as any others at FOA. For now, there were no more lectures about financial matters. Cromwell, maybe with the help of my parents, had a plan. He'd set the world right by vacuuming up dust balls and gum wrappers.

On Thursday, Giselle, Patrick, Mary, and Code-X gave Professor Eisenhower a truly rough ride in math. Eisenhower finally left class early completely flustered. It must have been the comments about his hair—the fact that he was only thirty and didn't have any left on his head. That was infinitely more interesting to the student body than math. Eisenhower, or Izzy as he was called behind his back, had been struggling with us all year. It wasn't a romp in the park for him, I'm sure. I mean, Cromwell had this mission thing going—trying to save us from oblivion. Prof. Dodd, P. Doodle as he was sometimes known, had his sense of dark humor to fall back on. Miss Marchand, of the quick wit and sexy long legs, taught a tolerable Biology class and when things got rough, she told stories about the adventures she had with her professional baseball playing boyfriends. Other part-time teachers came and went with the seasons. Cromwell would fill in when he was missing a faculty member. (More evidence that the school was falling apart in more ways than one.) But Eisenhower didn't seem to have the resilience needed to wrestle numbers into the heads of defective youth.

After Izzy left the room in a huff, Fin looked a little confused and I just sat back and closed my eyes. Code-X loved these kinds of scenes. He took to the front of the room, sat on the mahogany table that served as the teacher's desk. "How many of you think you'll make it to twenty-six?" he asked.

We laughed.

"No, I'm serious. Can you envision yourself out there in the world in your mid-twenties?"

The Code was high on something but that was nothing new. Giselle and Mary were giggling. He'd probably given them something too. What was his latest passion? I couldn't remember. Something over-the-counter, as I recall, but taken in doses beyond what was prescribed. Ryan seemed to have no trouble accessing drugs of many textures, sizes, and colors, whether they were over-the-counter or from what he called "street pharmacists."

"Give it up," I heard myself saying. All heads turned my way. I almost never spoke up in any class.

"Do I hear an opinion from the walking dead?"

"We're just a little tired of your rant, Ryan. None of us know what we'll be doing ten years from now. Some of us have a hard enough time making it through to the end of the day."

"My point exactly. Can you imagine yourself, Carson, waking one morning and you're, what, twenty-seven, twenty-eight, and like our esteemed math professor, Izzy

Eisenhower, you find your hair falling out? By the time you're thirty, your friends think your head has an odd likeness to a bowling ball?"

Code-X had a fairly limited IQ, I understood that. He had beaten all the rest of us when it came to how many schools had kicked him out. Six to be exact. As Ryan Luger, he had bad-mouthed teachers, done drugs, vandalized property, and gotten himself arrested for pissing on the sidewalk in the middle of a crowded street. When he changed his name to Code-X, he racked up the same inventory of petty offences but you could tell he wanted more out of life. He hoped to wreak more havoc.

The name came from an affinity he once had for codeine, but that had given way to harder drugs, "all recreational," as he put it. Cromwell kept trying to keep him clean, but Code had his ways. He was determined, one might assume, not to make it to twenty-six or maybe even twenty. Although he had a kind of demented cheerfulness to him, he truly didn't care what became of him.

I almost admired him for his attitude. He really didn't give a shit what anyone thought of him. Code was all about Code.

He never saw his parents, who were divorced, and living nearly a thousand miles away. They never came to visit, never called, and sent him to a "camp" once school was out for the summer. And, of course, they were among the deadbeats who weren't keeping up their payments for their son's bed and board or his education. It would seem that they just sent him spending money for recreational pills and weed and that was that.

Cromwell arrived as Code was giving us one of his little speeches about cocaine production in Colombia and how he had an "in" with a rebel group that had a billion dollar production facility there.

"And wouldn't Simon Bolivar be disappointed?" Dr. C. interjected, striding casually towards the front of the room like he wasn't mad at Code or any of us for crucifying our math teacher.

Ryan stayed seated on the mahogany table. "I suppose you want me to ask you who Simon Bolivar was."

"No need for that. I was about to tell you anyway. He was a revolutionary. Like many of you, he was born into a family of some wealth and had many assorted . . . influences." Cromwell noticed the vial of pills sitting on the table beside Ryan. He picked it up and studied the label.

"Prescription," Code said. "Call my doctor, if you want. He'll tell you it's a little something for stress." Code-X looked like the least stressed person on the planet. He seemed so relaxed in the state he was in that he was having a slightly hard time preventing himself from keeling over.

"I'll do just that," Crom said, pocketing the pills.

"Whatever," Code answered. "Simon Bolivar was particularly affected by the writings of the French philosopher Jean-Jacques Rousseau."

Ryan yawned and his yawn had a copycat effect on both Giselle and Mary, who probably shared Ryan's current body chemistry. I looked over at Fin, who seemed kind of fidgety. Fin never spoke up in class unless it was to ask to go to the bathroom.

"Never heard of him either," Ryan said, referring to the philosophical Frenchman.

Cromwell nodded and I could see that he was about to use this particular opportunity to put into practice his educational philosophy: use any opportunity to teach. Take any difficult situation and use it as a theater for imparting knowledge. One whiff of a Colombian drug lord and in a flash Dr. Crumples had turned it into a philosophy lesson.

"Rousseau believed that man's heyday, his high time"— and Cromwell exaggerated the word "high"—"his golden age, so to speak, was when he lived in a primitive state, a communal one. It was not perfect but there was a certain bond between man and man, man and nature which was quite wonderful."

"Was he a hippie?" Giselle wanted to know.

"No. He lived in the eighteenth century, wrote a few books, helped kick start the French Revolution, that sort of thing. He believed that if government should exist at all, it should exist at the pleasure and will of the people who create it. We would eventually call this democracy."

"He sounds like a hippie to me," Giselle said.

"Simon Bolivar took Rousseau's idea back to South America, where he led his people in a war of independence against the Spanish who ruled with an iron fist. And Bolivar succeeded. He envisioned a liberated and united South America but not everyone shared his vision. Separate nations formed: Bolivia, Venezuela, Peru, and Colombia. Bolivar was a true liberator but he was not loved by all. He died of tuberculosis at the age of forty-seven."

"Forty-seven is pretty old if you think about it," Code said.

"I'm fifty-two," Dr. Cromwell said. "What do you think it feels like to be fifty-two, Ryan?"

Ryan just shook his head. "I don't have the foggiest, man. I just know that I'll never be that old." Ryan looked more stoned than ever now. Could be that whatever he had taken was kicking in to the next level.

Cromwell surprised Ryan by gently grabbing him by both shoulders and looking him straight in the eye. "Ryan, I'll tell you what it feels like to be fifty-two years old. Fifty-two rocks."

And with that, Cromwell let go of Ryan's shoulders, stood up and left the room.

Maybe he had some more vacuuming to do. Or perhaps there were dishes to be washed.

Chapter Ten

The school was starting to feel more and more claustrophobic these days. The weather was getting warmer and all I could think about was *not* sitting around in my room with Fin glued to his computer. I know I've said that the school was the only place in the world where I felt I could survive. I don't really mean to say that I liked it or anything, it's just that I felt I could tolerate it. Yet the place drove me crazy with all those neurotic, whacked-out kids and, of course, I was one of them. But if I couldn't crawl out of myself, I could occasionally escape from the madhouse.

What I wanted most out of life maybe was to be someone other than me. I wanted *out* of myself. But I couldn't find the instruction book. So I knew that wasn't going to happen.

There were small green leaves on the big hardwood trees now. Some of the old elm tree trunks were still standing. Dutch elm disease, they say, had killed them but their massive remains still looked imposing if bleak there against all the new growth.

The grass was green on the lawns. There were birds singing. Don't think I'm going to get soppy and sentimental about all this. I'm just saying I noticed it and it was why I was out walking again after classes. My feet were headed, of their own accord, down to the wharf. I took my jacket off and breathed in the air. There might have been flowers up and maybe even blooming somewhere. I don't know. I thought I smelled something like that but I wasn't fully paying attention.

What I was thinking was this: someday, this will all be gone. No more leaves, no more green, no more smell of flowers. If not today, tomorrow. We will screw this up badly. I touched one of the big elm trees just then. I put my hand flat on its rough surface. I found myself stopping and putting both hands on it now, making some kind of weird personal contact with a big, hulking, dead stump of a tree. I looked skyward into its gnarled, leafless, dead and haunted branches.

I knew it wasn't people in this case that had killed the elm trees. Some kind of bug or disease. Hundred-year-old tree wiped out by something very tiny. And so it goes. Maybe that would be what would get us, all of us, before we had a chance to reduce the planet to ash. Maybe some little bug would come along and relieve us of all our suffering.

I let go of the tree just as a couple of younger boys were walking by. They stared the way kids do and I gave them a threatening look, and then kicked the air to intimidate them. It worked. They ran.

At the wharf, a couple of the smaller fishing boats were in. The tide was high and the boat decks were closer to dock level. I sat on a crate and watched as a couple of fishermen slit the throats and bellies of large silvery fish. They hacked off the heads and threw them to gulls flying overhead, which caught them as they dipped low in the sky. Sometimes, the fishermen just heaved the unwanted fish guts over the side of the boat into the clear waters beneath. It was all rather satisfying to watch.

The sun was out and the light reflected off the sharp knives used to gut the fish. The air was warm and there was a rank fish smell in the air (surprise, surprise). I watched with some fascination as men in slimy rubber aprons tossed fish heads and entrails into the air and over the side into the water beneath. I looked out far across the inlet to the shore on the other side. It appeared remote, hazy, and otherworldly. I listened to the men talking about their lives. And for a brief instant, I started feeling like things weren't so bad.

I need to confess that I didn't trust the feeling I had just then. It wasn't that I was really feeling good or okay or anything like that. It was just that, right then, I don't think I gave a crap about anything. If you've been there, you know this feeling. It's a rare one for me and it never lasts. Time is like this boat that you are on. You can't see who is steering it but it is taking you to weird unknown and sometimes awful or terrifying places. You don't have a life jacket and you can't just jump off. You can't see where you came from or where you are going. There's no one to ask. You've tried. You don't know if you are going to crash into a submerged rock, sink, and drown, or if you'll end up somewhere safe on a further shore. All you know is that you are stuck here with no way out.

And then suddenly the engine stops and you are dead in the water. The gulls are swirling, the sky is blue, and you are still alone. But you don't care. You have stopped and that is all that matters. And there is air to breathe.

That's what it felt like.

But it didn't last. It never does.

A young guy in overalls, about nineteen, walked my way with a cigarette dangling from his mouth. "Got a light?" he asked.

"Nope."

For some reason, he didn't walk away. He just stood there staring at me. "Seen you down here before. Couldn't figure you out."

"What's to figure?" I asked.

"Saw you with that girl. Christine."

"So?"

He laughed, held his unlit cigarette up to the sky. "Now there's a good time," he said with a smirk on his face.

"Screw you," I said and got up to leave.

"What's your problem?" I heard him say as I walked off. I half expected him to grab me or something but he didn't. I just kept on walking.

I decided to go bother Mel but he had a sign on his door saying he'd be back in thirty minutes. Probably down at the liquor store.

The calm I had experienced was all gone. Now I felt like I had ants crawling around in my brain. Maybe that's why Ryan had decided that being high as often as possible was preferable to dealing with life straight. Maybe that's why Mel decided to stay sloshed and hole up in his bookstore. Maybe everyone was trying to avoid this feeling of confusion and rage that was part of everyday life.

Walking up Main Street, I noticed the waiter from Alfredo's standing outside on the sidewalk smoking a cigarette. He just kept staring at me as I walked towards him. I should have just walked right by him but instead I stopped.

"What are you looking at?" I asked.

He blew smoke out through his mouth, straight at me. "Just wondering why you keep coming down here into town. Isn't it pretty clear you and your other friends at that so-called school aren't wanted here?"

I realized just then that the guy had finally come out and said what everyone else in town was thinking. It made my blood boil. "Asshole," I said to him straight up. I could have hit him but I didn't.

• • •

As I walked on, I kicked over a couple of big plastic trash cans and spilled their contents onto the sidewalk. No one said anything to me but when I shoved over a third one, I noticed one of those guys in uniform who gives out parking tickets. He saw me do it and watched as I walked on. Although he wasn't exactly a cop, he could probably get me in trouble. I picked up my pace and headed out of town up the hill. All I could think about was that maybe Christine would have a beer for me, one of those high alcohol German beers. I could get a little buzz on, pretend the world wasn't as fucked up as it was.

Somebody was working on an old rusty Honda in a neighbor's yard. There were dogs barking. The gravel road had plenty of spring potholes and all the front yards (if you could call them that) were rutted and muddy. Some kids played on broken swing sets and I heard country music playing loudly through a window. Some stupid song with a guy singing that he couldn't tell the difference "between Iran and Iraq." And he seemed to be bragging about his ignorance. I don't know why that lyric stuck with me but it did.

Christine's trailer looked like something old, defeated, and forgotten. The neighbors watched me as I knocked loudly on the flimsy aluminum screen door.

No answer. Damn.

I should have just turned around and left, gone back to the school. But I didn't. I banged more loudly.

A woman from inside a nearby trailer yelled through her window, "I haven't seen her. I don't think she's home."

But I knocked this time on the window. "Christine. It's Carson." Good plan: announce yourself to the trailer trash neighbors and hope you piss someone off enough to come after you with a tire iron. Dogs barked more loudly. The wind seemed to be shifting around to the north and I felt a chill. I just stood there, waiting.

I tried the storm door and the catch on the handle was so worn that it opened even though I think it had been locked. The real door behind it didn't even have a handle. I pushed it gently and it opened. But I didn't go in.

"Christine?"

"Go away," I head a voice say.

"Why?" I shouted back. The neighbors were plenty interested now. Must have been commercial time for the soaps.

"Just go away," she said. This was the voice of a girl with a problem, a big problem. It suddenly occurred to me that she might be in there with someone. A guy maybe. What business was it of mine, anyhow? I felt a wave of confusion sweep over me. Why couldn't I just walk away? She made her point. She didn't want to see me. Damn.

"I just wanted to ask you something," I said matter-of-factly.

A few seconds later she appeared at the open door. She had on those old dirty jeans and the flannel shirt that wasn't tucked in. Her hair was a mess and the look on her face . . . well, she looked scared. She stood back from the door. She sure wasn't inviting me in.

"You okay?" I asked.

She wasn't. "What did you want to ask?"

"I wanted to know if you have any more beer." I whispered so the neighbors wouldn't hear. "I'd like to buy one from you."

She put her hand on her hip. "What do you think I am, a bootlegger?"

"Can I come in?" I was feeling really uneasy with the neighbors watching.

"No."

"Why?"

"Because."

Then I said something that shocked me. "I thought we were friends," I said like it was straight out of some cheesy TV sitcom.

"Are you some kind of freak?" she asked, like I had just done something to offend her.

"Are you all right?" I blurted out.

"I don't know," she said.

"Well, you . . . um . . . seemed okay at dinner the other night. That was a truly strange scene."

"I liked it," she said angrily. "But it was a mistake, dammit."

"I don't understand."

"Don't they teach you anything at your stupid school?" she asked and walked away from the door. I heard her open the refrigerator. It wasn't exactly an invitation but I grabbed the door frame and hoisted myself up into the trailer, avoiding the broken metal step.

Chapter Eleven

It was gloomy inside with all the window shades pulled down. Christine was holding one of those tall cans of beer out to me and she was already drinking from one herself.

"What don't I understand?" I ventured.

She cleared off some magazines from the torn furniture and sat down. I picked a kitchen chair and sat down, holding my cold can of beer between my hands.

"Your mother and father. They were nice. It was awful."

"It wasn't my idea."

"Well, I had forgotten what it was like . . . to have parents, I mean. Maybe I never even knew what it was like. All I remember was screaming and yelling and sometimes them hitting each other. I remember one leaving or the other. I remember my father splitting and then coming back and me thinking everything would be okay. But it never was okay. I kept thinking, someday, somehow, it was all going to turn out all right. That my family would be like other families. But it wasn't."

I took a deep slug of beer. "Every family has problems."

"Not like mine. Being there with your parents being nice to me, a complete stranger, made me realize how much I've been cheated out of."

"We have problems too, believe me," I said.

"Yeah," she said bitterly, "like what? Your father squeezes the toothpaste from the wrong end? Or your brother doesn't put the toilet seat down? What kind of problems do you guys have?"

"The problem is me," I admitted. "Every damn thing they did for me, I screwed up somehow. *They* were just fine. I was the worst thing that could have happened to my family."

She didn't know what to say. Suddenly she was angrier. She got up and walked to me, looked me hard in the eyes. I could see now that she'd been crying and that maybe she hadn't slept in a long time. "You have it all. How can you screw that up? What is wrong with you?"

I swallowed some more beer and didn't know what to say. Maybe I almost laughed a small cynical laugh and in a low, unemotional tone, I said, "I hate the world and everything in it."

"What does that mean?"

"It's what I wrote on my English essay. I think I meant it."

"You're messed up, you know that?"

"Yeah, I do. And that's part of why I feel so bad. I'm not just my own problem. My parents are stuck with me, too. At least at the school, I don't have to inflict myself on them."

"They seemed happy to see you," she said.

"They're my parents. If I was a mass murderer, they'd still be happy to see me. That's who they are. You know how difficult that is to live with?"

Somehow this had made her angry again. I saw rage in her eyes. And then she slapped me. Hard across the cheek.

I wasn't about to hit a girl. But it hurt and I didn't know why she did it. When she reached out her arm and I realized she was about to smack me again, I grabbed both her wrists and held on tight. "I'll scream," she said.

"Go ahead." At that point, I really didn't care. I was confused and angry, angrier than I'd been in a long while. And I didn't even understand what was going on.

The sleeves hung loose on the arms of her flannel shirt. At the wrists they were unbuttoned. I gripped harder onto her arms and held them up to the dim light. The scars. Dozens of them. Like someone had drilled holes in her arms. She saw me staring. I had no idea what I was dealing with. Both arms had the scars.

"God," I said, still holding onto her, afraid to let go. "What have you been doing to yourself?" I was thinking drugs, shooting hard drugs into veins, but there were so many scars. I didn't understand.

"You couldn't understand."

"No, I don't think I could. Tell me anyway."

"It's none of your business." She twisted her arms now and I knew I couldn't keep holding her like this. I realized I was hurting her.

"Okay, I'll leave."

"No," she said, suddenly softening, sitting back on the vinyl chair, sitting down on top of some old ripped *Cosmopolitan* magazines. "Even if I say it out loud, it wouldn't make any sense. Not to you. Not to me."

I decided to say nothing. Part of me so much wanted to run but it was like the life had drained out of me. I didn't have the energy to leave, to walk back to the school.

"It's all right. I don't want to know." I really didn't.

"My mother called yesterday to say she isn't coming back. She's with Mick, the drummer. A gig somewhere on the west coast. Her exact words were, 'It's all too good to be true.'"

"She sounds like a real sweet mom."

"I actually think she was at one time. Then things just started going wrong. She and my dad had been fighting for years. The cops came sometimes. Usually they made up. Finally my dad left."

"Someone he met on the Internet?" I ventured.

"We didn't have a computer. Someone he met at the gas station."

"Pretty much the same thing. Did you love him?"

"Sure," she said. "When I was little, he was good to me. I think he really was. At least that's the way I remember it. When he left, he said he was doing it for me. He was doing me a favor."

"Bullshit."

"That's what I said."

"You hear from him?"

"Card at Christmas. Postcard maybe once in a while."

"You're gonna have quite a collection once your mom starts sending you news."

"Shithead," she said with the barest hint of a smile.

"Loser," I shot back.

It was a way of breaking the treacherous seriousness of it all. She understood the code. It worked. She told me more.

"Me and my mom were stuck here in this dump for years. She waitressed but she hated it. She had even worked at Alfredo's for a while, but they fired her when she got caught taking leftover food home instead of dumping it in the trash."

"To hire Snotnose there, I guess. Did you hate him or what?"

"Hated him and his family and everyone he ever liked."

"My sentiments exactly. Although I don't think he had many friends. My guess was that he was a cadaver. You don't have to pay the dead a very high wage. My father wasted a tip on him. I wish I could have talked him out of that. Meanwhile, back to your mother."

"Social Services got involved. Lucky for the world, I was an only child. We were on welfare here and there. Mom had a way with men. Boyfriends came and went. When I'd come home, I'd check to see what kind of shoes were left inside the door. A couple of times I was put in a foster home, but then nobody wanted me because I was too old. There were a couple of awful group homes. That's when I started this."

This referred to her arms. I decided not to ask again. "How'd you end up back here?"

She threw up her arms. "Either my mother took me back or they would have put me in some kind of institution. I pretended to be normal. I pretended to be okay. I even started going to school regularly.

"When she'd leave, sometimes I thought it was because she wanted to escape from me and my problems. I actually thought it was my fault. My mom said she felt bad about leaving. I really think she did. I remember her saying, 'I'm a complete failure as a mother. I'm sorry.' That's what she said. And you know what?"

"What?"

"She was right. So when she saw her way out, leaving with the Mick guy—him with his snoring and his big beer belly and that beat-up van of his—well, she took her one-way ticket out of here."

"How could she do that?"

"She said I was going to be seventeen in a couple of months anyway. Then I'd be 'legal.' I understood what that means. Mainly that Social Services wouldn't get involved. And that she could be free and clear of me if she wanted. At least that's the way she put it."

"At least you have a place to live," I offered, trying to help her see that there was some glimmer of hope.

She took a slug of beer and kind of snorted. "Rent's paid until the end of the month. Then, guess what? I'm truly on my own."

"You rented this place?" For some reason it didn't occur to me that people actually rented dumps like this.

"Maybe I'll just move up to something a bit more comfortable," she said, the edge back in her voice. "This all sounds like something made up to you, doesn't it?"

"No," I said softly. "I want to help."

"There's nothing you can do."

I didn't want to admit that she was right. What could I do? There was nothing I could do to help. "Maybe my parents . . ." I began.

"Leave your parents out of this. Trust me. I've been down the road with do-gooders trying to help me. It doesn't work.

The system kicks in. You know what I mean. *The* system. You can call it what you like, but the system will come to the aid of your well-meaning parents and I'll end up in some institution. So don't even think about it."

I believed her and understood exactly how it could be. Whatever anyone did to try to help, it only ended up making things worse. She was crying now and I felt I was to blame. The beer had kicked in and I felt my eyes stinging. I held her arms again, this time more gently, and I stared at the healed wounds. I realized now they were too big to be needle marks. It was something else. "Can you tell me about this?" I asked softly.

She shook her head no. "Not yet. It's so hard to explain. Even I don't understand. Will you hold me?" she whispered.

"Yes," I said. And I held her to me, feeling her warmth, feeling the weight of all the sadness in the world gathered there in my arms on that spring afternoon.

"Let's get outta here for a while," I said. "Have you been outside today?"

"No."

"You didn't go to school?"

"I don't really go to school."

"You quit?"

"I just stopped going. For a while I'd pretend to be in school and show up maybe once or twice a week. But it wasn't worth it. School was full of creeps."

"The People of the Turds."

"What?"

"The lads with cow-pies on the soles of their feet."

Christine smiled, almost laughing, but she sucked it back in. It was like she couldn't let herself smile or even feel good for a second.

"On the wharf, one of your classmates—probably—started giving me a hard time for no reason at all. Had the IQ of a piss clam, is my guess. He really ticked me off. I can see what you're saying."

"Carson, what about you? Why don't you live at home?"

"Fucked-up rich kids go to fucked-up rich kids' school. Believe me, I'm better off where I'm at. And don't tell me how nice my parents are again. I know they're nice. If it weren't for me, my family would be the ones you see when you buy a photo frame in Wal-Mart. Happy, smiling, home people. It's really too bad that people buy that frame and replace the perfect family with a photo-shopped version of their own dysfunctional brood."

"Dysfunctional?"

"You never heard that word?"

She permitted one small laugh, just a tiny one, and then crumpled the empty beer can for effect. "I heard that word a lot—from the social workers, from the counsellors. But I never heard it from a kid."

"Hey, I'm sixteen. I'm not a kid. I know everything I need to know."

"But you're smart, right? Really smart?"

"Brains don't amount to a hill of beans in this world," I said, misquoting somebody I once saw in an old film.

"Do you think I'm smart?"

"I don't know. Are you?"

"I thought I was once. But I was terrible in school."

"Do you read?"

"Sometimes. Mostly magazines."

"Magazines suck."

"What do you read?" she asked.

"History stuff."

"Get out."

"No. I like to read about wars and things like that. The more I read, the more I realize how totally wasted we are. We are scum. We evolve from scum and you'd think we'd wise up, but the evidence shows that isn't the case. We started out as slime out there in the ocean somewhere. We get zapped by lightning and, before you know it, we're putting men on the moon. But deep down, we still think like, um . . . lizards, I think it is. The reptile part of our brain is what holds us back. Greed, lust, territorial pursuit." I paused for effect. It'd been a long while since I had waxed eloquent about what a retrograde species we were. "I've decided to opt out of the human race once I grow up," I said smugly.

"Can I join you?" Christine asked and it gave me a chill. I think I blushed just then. It was the nicest thing anyone had said to me in a long while.

"I gotta get you out of here for some fresh air," I said, shaking my head.

• • •

We walked out of the trailer park and downhill to town. "I want to introduce you to someone."

"One of the turd people?"

"No. Someone different."

There was silence between us and I was suddenly aware

of our breathing. And then something else. "Did you hear that?" I asked.

She looked at me with those hurt eyes. "Hear what?" She could look me in the eye now, and I again studied the sorrow there and the darkness in the skin beneath her eyes. I nearly tripped, not looking where I was going.

"The birds," I said. It was spring and birds were chirping. "But I don't know anything about birds so I can't tell you what kind of bird it is."

Her eyes changed. She gave me a goofy look. "You never heard a sparrow before?"

"How did you know it was a sparrow?"

"Tiny, ordinary-looking bird with a big voice."

"I don't see it anywhere."

"Probably long gone by now. They fly fast."

"A sparrow," I repeated. I'd never even thought about sparrows before.

"I'm putting it on my list."

"Which list is that?" I asked.

"Of things I like."

"So the sparrow is right up there with the seaweed at the bottom of the harbor?"

"Right."

"Big list. Two things."

"No, three," she said.

I didn't ask her what the third thing was. But I had a hopeful hunch.

• • •

The little bell went off when we walked into Mel's bookstore. My guess had been correct about Mel's afternoon foray to the liquor store. What was left of his hair was in a kind of wild mess, like he'd had his hands on an electrostatic generator all afternoon.

"Carson, good to see you," he said. "I've been reading the most extraordinary stuff. And it's right down your alley." He hadn't seen Christine behind me but I knew better than to stop him when he was on a tear.

Mel picked up a thick, dusty volume that had been on the counter in front of him. He took a sip from his ever-present "coffee." "Imagine," he began, "that it is 1915 and you are a soldier, a German soldier of the air, and you have the technology of flight—zeppelins, to be precise. Now listen to this direct quote from Captain Ernst Lehman recounting his time with the German zeppelin service. 'The idea was to equip from twelve to twenty zeppelins and drill their crews to function as a coordinated task force. Each ship would carry about three hundred firebombs. They would attack simultaneously at night.'" He paused for another sip. Christine hung back quietly behind me. Mel never even looked up.

Licking his lips he flipped through some pages and said, "And now, here's the good part, this time from one Captain Peter Strasser who was head of the German navy's airship division, and I quote, 'We who strike the enemy where his heart beats have been slandered as *baby killers* and *murderers of women*. What we do is repugnant to us too, but necessary. Very necessary . . . modern warfare is total warfare.'"

Mel looked up at us now, his eyes ablaze with booze and the horrors of military history. He was about to go on a rant similar to my recent diatribe about what a loathsome batch of intelligent scum we humans were, but then he noticed Christine.

"What are you doing here?" he snarled.

Christine tucked herself behind me. I didn't understand the connection.

"What's wrong?" I ask Mel. "She's my friend." It wasn't a word I'd heard myself say in a long, long while and it tripped haltingly off my lips.

"She's a thief," Mel shouted.

"Let's go," Christine said.

Mel moved from around the counter and began walking, or should I say *weaving*, in a kind of alcoholic dance towards us. He was still gripping his book. Christine was inching backwards towards the door.

"Wait," I said to both of them. I turned to Christine. "Did you steal something from Mel?"

Mel blurted out, "She was in here and stole a book. She thought I wasn't looking."

"Two books actually," Christine said.

Mel's furry eyebrows flared. "No one steals my books." With the fury in him, he could have dropped zeppelin firebombs on all of the book thieves of the world.

"I'm sorry," Christine said. "I didn't have any money."

Mel tethered the zeppelin overhead and didn't light any fuses. "What did you steal?"

"*Catcher in the Rye*. It was only a paperback."

"And?" Mel was shouting now.

"*One Flew Over the Cuckoo's Nest*. They're both kind of beat-up but I'll return them."

Mel seemed to be counting his teeth with his tongue.

When he concluded the assessment, he said, "No. Keep them. I have more. Just don't steal anything today."

"I promise," she said.

And it was as if that part of the conversation had never happened. He returned to the counter, fiddled with some keys on the old cash register. "That letter from the honorable Captain Strasser. That was to his mother. I failed to point that out."

"Was she proud of her son?" I asked.

Mel looked puzzled. "I don't know. This book only has his correspondence. They did drop firebombs on London, though. Quite a few of them. It was all new technology and tons of fun for men like Strasser and Lehman and their good pal Captain Heinrich Mathy who dropped his load of death, sixty-five bombs or so, on the unwary Londoners that fine September day of 1915. One even dropped just outside the Dolphin Pub on Red Lion Street. Inside, unwary Londoners were having their evening pint. The fun came to an end when the front of the pub blew in and killed the lot of them." And then he looked up at Christine again. "What did you say your name was?"

"Christine."

He walked menacingly towards her and suddenly held out the book. "Take this home and study it. Come back and tell me what you think."

Christine blinked and then looked at me. I nodded and shrugged my shoulders. I think it had been a long while since anyone had given her a gift, even if it was a book about military death and destruction during the early part of the twentieth century.

Chapter Twelve

I guess Fin had, in his own curious way, become accustomed to having me in the room with him even though his attention was usually drawn to the computer screen. My absence from his social life—and I was pretty much his entire social life as his roommate—had made him even more withdrawn than usual. The bond, if you could call it that, between Griffin and me was that we were both avowed misanthropes. Yes, misanthrope. Let me explain.

• • •

Dr. Cromwell had visited us once in our room early on when it was becoming obvious that neither Fin nor I were the slightest bit interested in any of the extracurricular activities like after-school basketball (an exhausting waste of physical energy), improv theater group (really just a cover for psychological counselling), pizza parties, art group (more therapy masked as hobby), nature walks, or, the worst of the worst, that torturous event called "peer counselling."

No one was forced to do anything extracurricular. In reality, no one was forced to do anything at Flunk Out A. And some of us took advantage of the Doc's liberal education notions to hone our skills at being lazy and sluggish and preparing ourselves to be non-productive, useless, reclusive members of society. Yet, for unknown reasons, Fin and I usually went to classes. The main attraction there was watching our teachers suffer through the sorry job of trying to educate the wankers who were our classmates.

At any rate, early on, upon noting Fin's and my own reclusive nature, Dr. Crumpet made a house call on us late one afternoon. Fin was hunkered down over his keyboard trying to communicate with one of his Internet friends, a young terrorist in Chechnya, and I was reading a book on medieval torture that Mel had sold to me at half price.

"You two should really think about getting involved in at least one after-school activity."

"Fin and I don't really like being around people any more than we have to." I spoke for both of us. Fin nodded his approval.

"Don't like people, huh?" Dr. C. stroked his chin. "Ever hear of a French chap named Molière? "

"Let me guess. He didn't like people either."

"Not exactly that. He was a writer and around the middle of the seventeenth century he wrote a play called *The Misanthrope*."

"Never heard of it. You, Fin?"

Fin shook his head no. Fin didn't really know a whole heck of a lot about anything outside of his narrow area of expertise.

"A misanthrope," Cromwell continued unabated, "is a person who hates people. Molière would have said it is someone who hates 'mankind.'"

"Plenty of good reasons for that," I said.

"Agreed. And had Monsieur Molière been here in this room today, he would have had a bracing little chat with both of you on the subject. Molière's character, the misanthrope, despises what he sees as deceit, hypocrisy, and falsehood all around him."

"So does he lock himself away in his room or what?"

"Oddly enough, he doesn't. He goes out into the world and tries to live according to his principles of complete and total honesty in all his dealings with people."

"But I thought he hated dealing with people."

"He hated the foibles of mankind and so hoped to change society."

"Through being honest?" I couldn't help it but I laughed. Fin mimicked me and laughed too, an annoying habit of his, this copycat thing.

"Right."

"And where did it get him?"

"Pretty much nowhere. It didn't work. The play was a comedy about how poorly honesty works in dealing with people. He failed abysmally, this misanthrope."

Cromwell saw the puzzled looks on our faces. As usual, the sly old headmaster of our beloved school had surreptitiously given us a small lesson in literature. Molière, seventeenth century, *The Misanthrope*. But there seemed to be no real great moral lesson.

"So what you two students have here is a kind of misanthropic club. You avoid people because you find them what? Shallow? Hypocritical? False?"

"Among other things," I said. "But you pretty much get

the picture."

"Let's refer to your after-school activities then as meetings of the Molière Club."

"I'd rather not," I said.

"Just think about it." Cromwell pointed towards Fin's computer screen with its screen saver, an aerial photograph of Nagasaki after the Americans had dropped the second (and completely unnecessary) nuclear bomb. "Go on the Internet and see if you can find other misanthropic societies or movements. It's not a pretty picture but you should be well-versed in what you believe in. I've always felt that if there is anything worth doing, you should do it to the best of your abilities. Even being a misanthrope."

Cromwell slapped his thighs and stood up, strangely pleased with himself. This was the thing about Dr. C. You always knew he was messing with your head but, afterwards, you didn't really mind it. He was always trying to make you feel okay about yourself and he never got frustrated or flustered no matter how ignorant or inattentive any of his students were to him. But now I had a word for what I was: misanthropic. Maybe I could make a low-budget movie of my life and call it: *I was a Teenage Misanthrope*.

"What do you suppose that was all about?" Fin asked after Cromwell left, acting as if he had not understood a word.

I shrugged. "Dunno," I said. "You know what Dr. Crom is like."

"Yeah, I know," he said and went back to his chat room. I wanted to ask him if he heard from his parents but I knew that he probably hadn't and it would only make him feel bad. I suppose that if no one had invented the Internet, his mom and dad might still be together and guys like Griffin might have to go out into the world and down to the Harborville Library to find out about renegade uranium. I felt bad for the guy, I really did.

"I read in the paper," I said, "about a man who claims that Hitler's scientists were pretty close to coming up with their own nuclear bomb not long before Germany was defeated."

Fin smiled. "That would have been the end of the world as we know it."

I had triggered a little game we played once in a while— tossing back and forth the possible ways the planet could be wrecked. Fin cleared his throat. "I found out on the Internet that one of those rocks the astronauts brought back from the moon—well, they discovered it had some deadly virus that if exposed to air would spread and kill off seventy-five percent or more of the human race. So they have to keep it in a sealed container forever."

"And if the container ever leaks it would be TEOTWAWKI," I responded. Shorthand. Fin understood. "That would be disappointing, though, if the virus was set free," I said, "because there is an asteroid the size of Connecticut that is headed towards earth although it might take seventy-five to a hundred years to get here. They say it won't crash right into the earth but come close enough to tear away most of the earth's atmosphere. They say we'll die from asphyxiation and shortly thereafter the sun will burn everything off the face of the planet."

"TEOTWAWKI," Fin said with a goofy grin on his face.

Chapter Thirteen

In the same way that pieces of the old Farnsworth mansion kept falling off, it was becoming more and more obvious that the school itself was being chipped away bit by bit and might soon collapse entirely. We were getting used to seeing Dr. Cromwell vacuuming or even cleaning up the bathrooms in the evenings. Mr. Eisenhower had given up on us, seemingly given up on mathematics and education altogether, and taken a sales job at a place called Wacky Wheatley's that sold discount video game equipment and wide-screen TVs.

Cromwell explained Eisenhower's disappearance as a "mid-career vocational shift." We were aware that he had been fed up with trying to teach the sorry lot of us for a long time and I suppose that, when his latest cheque bounced, he decided to spend his waking hours doing something more meaningful like selling mindless entertainment electronics to the masses. It was his loss.

Despite the advancing warmth and the green days (for those of us who ventured outdoors), a pall of gloom hung over the academy. Could it be that it was really on its last legs? I had this haunting fear that June would roll around, we'd all be shipped back to home or other stables for the summer, and Farnsworth would itself fade into history. The building itself, now probably only held together by some physical force field created by our beloved leader, would disintegrate and sift into the ground. I was more than a little angry that those well-to-do tight-ass parents were still not willing to pay their sons' and daughters' tardy tuition.

I picked up the house phone and made a rare call home. My mom answered, sounding both shocked and delighted. "Carson, is everything okay?"

"I'm okay, if that's what you mean."

"Well, it's good to hear your voice. We really enjoyed having dinner with you and your friend. Is she . . . is she okay?"

My mom thought that begging for money on the street was a sign of something not going well in a teenager's life. "She just does that for attention," I lied. "Some kids do that. Don't worry, she's okay." I didn't want my do-good mother snooping around into Christine's life and ending up with Social Services getting involved. That would be a disaster. "I'm calling about the school," I said. "You guys paid my tuition and room and board, right?"

"It was paid in full the first day of your school year."

I suspected as much. My parents were the world's most responsible people. And that was part of why I was such a big disappointment to them. "Well, a lot of the other parents still haven't paid. I think the school is in deep trouble," I said.

"We know that. Your father and I made some phone calls on behalf of Dr. Cromwell. He's not at all good at asking for money. But he has the soul of an angel."

"So what's with the deadbeat parents?"

"We were appalled," my mom said. "We really were. I think a few might have sent in cheques after we reminded them of their responsibilities. But some of them were downright rude."

"They have their kids at Farnsworth but refuse to pay?"

"One father threatened to pull his son out. He said he'd never been so insulted in his life. He was indignant and downright nasty and said he'd rather just send the boy someplace else. He made it sound like it was a dog of his that he was keeping at a kennel."

She wouldn't tell me whose father it was but she didn't really have to. This was Ryan's old man. I could tell it was the breeding stock that Code had come from. Maybe that was why he had stopped being Ryan and had converted himself to Code-X.

"I'm not sure there *is* another place for a lot of these kids to go."

"Then why wouldn't their parents pay what they owe?"

What my mother didn't understand was that she was asking this question of a misanthrope. "Because they are assholes," I wanted to say. But didn't.

Talking to my mom made me feel both homesick and guilty. I felt bad that I had hurt them the way I did over the years. They didn't really do anything to deserve me. And whatever it was that was wrong with me, it was my fault—not anybody else's. I just believed that I could never fit properly into this world. I think I must have been born angry. Even when I was young, I'd say mean things to other kids to hurt their feelings. It was like this: if I couldn't figure out how to be happy, then I'd do my best to make others feel bad.

My parents did everything right. But every time I had a chance to screw up, I took the opportunity. I stole things from other kids even when I was little. It wasn't that I needed anything. I just took things because I thought I could get away with it. I had hated most of my teachers and they hated me right back. And it's tough to get a good grade from a teacher you've trained to hate your guts. It really is.

My little brother was like my parents: he too did everything right. He played it by the book and when I realized the game he was up to, that made me even madder. And nastier. To him and to everyone else around me. By hating so many people, I did a fine job of training me to hate myself. It's possible that Cromwell was beginning to understand a few of these basic things about me but I wasn't about to let him think he understood what made me tick.

"Carson, honey," my mom said, "do you want to come home? Is that what this is about?"

I was really glad there was no one in the room just then. My eyes began to burn. And I started to cry. As soon as I began to cry I felt angrier than ever. I felt the rage in my belly first. I was sucking my lower lip and offering up nothing but silence to her question.

"Carson, you still there?'

I fought for control of my voice. The last thing I wanted was to go home. I knew I couldn't survive there. I was certain of it. "No, that's not it," I said. "I like it here. I'm just worried about the school."

"We love you, Carson. Your father, brother, and I miss you a lot. We just want you to be happy." I could tell that she was sniffing back her own tears now. I'd heard her say this a thousand times before.

And each time she did, it only made me feel worse. "Bye, Mom."

"Bye Carson. Thanks for calling. Be good."

• • •

It was dinnertime and everyone else was in the small cafeteria eating the food prepared by Mrs. Chin. Although I had thought at first that she was Chinese, I had later learned that she was Vietnamese. I'd never learned her whole story—no one at the school had—but from what I could piece together, Dr. Cromwell sponsored her and her nephew as refugees quite a few years back and she came here to work at the school. She had a prosthesis for one leg. It was made from plastic. She lost her real leg to a land mine. She didn't like talking about it. But she never complained. Mrs. Chin lost most of her family somehow as well. Something to do with leaving her home on a boat with other refugees. Some of them survived, some didn't. The old woman with one leg survived.

Ryan and Patrick could be pretty nasty to Mrs. Chin. She didn't seem to care. I understood that she was totally loyal to Dr. C. I'd even heard her arguing with him. She insisted that he not do any of the cleaning, that the students should not see him doing housework. But he would not let her do it.

Mrs. Chin took her cooking job very seriously. Everyone complained about the food but it wasn't because the food was bad. Mrs. Chin couldn't satisfy everyone. Once, after everyone had finished eating and left the dining room, I saw Mrs. Chin sit down to eat some of what she'd cooked for the students. With chopsticks in hand, she ate all alone beneath the old dusty chandelier. I sometimes wondered what would have become of Mrs. Chin if there had never been a war in her country and if she had not lost her leg and her family.

• • •

I sat down outside the main entrance under the portico by the crumbling concrete pillars. I sat on the cold, sweating bricks and looked at the daffodils that had come up through unraked leaves and the empty, tossed chip bags and candy wrappers. I looked up at the new leaves on the trees and at the blue sky beyond. And then I looked at the grass. Once upon a time this had been a well-manicured lawn. In days gone by, there had probably been full-time gardeners to clip the hedges, collect the dead leaves, weed the garden, and mow the lawns. Already, early in the season, the grass was tall and ragged looking. I stared at the lawn for a long while, my eyes still burning as if I'd been standing over a campfire. And then I had this overwhelming desire.

Cromwell was in his office with a lot of paperwork on his desk. Bills, I think. He had an exasperated look on his face. One I'd never seen before, but I knew that whatever grief there was in Doc's life, he repaired himself in front of a mirror each time before presenting himself to his students. I could envision him staring into that mirror and rearranging his countenance before going downstairs and assuring every one of us that it was all under control.

But now he had to do a quick fix on that frown as I had just knocked once and walked right in.

"You got a mower?" I asked him.

"Excuse me?"

"A lawn mower. I want to mow the grass."

Dr. Cromwell was puzzled. He set down some papers and blinked hard as if I had just spoken to him in a foreign language. Perhaps he thought he was hallucinating.

"I'd really like to mow the lawn," I said. "Is there a mower anywhere? Gas?"

"According to your mother, you have allergies," he said. "Pollen, dust, grass."

I did have allergies. It was all in my medical files. "You must be mixing me up with someone else."

Cromwell scratched under his chin and scrutinized me. "You want to mow?"

"The grass needs cutting. Have you noticed?"

"No," he said. "I wasn't paying attention."

"If you don't mow the lawn, the neighbors might start complaining."

The Farnsworth neighbors complained about everything. In their million-dollar-plus houses, they were despondent about the wreckage of a tumbledown academy for flunk outs in their midst. Cromwell fielded their phone complaints, dutifully endured the lectures of health inspectors and town councillors, and had even been taken to court for having "unsightly premises." It must all have been most humbling.

"Mrs. Chin can show you where the mower is," he said at length.

"Mrs. Chin?"

"Yes."

• • •

Mrs. Chin studied me when I asked her about the mower. "Why you want to do this thing, now?" she asked.

"It just needs to be done. I'm volunteering to do it."

She smiled; I had almost never seen her smile. She patted me on the top of the head. "Come. I show you how to start it."

Mrs. Chin led me out to the garage. I followed her as she walked. There was no limp at all and I couldn't figure out which was her real leg and which one was fake. As the garage door was lifted, squirrels went running from side to side on the stained concrete floor. Like everything else at Farnsworth, the garage was a disaster. Dead leaves had blown in and there were old tires piled in the corners. A couple of glass panes were broken and the place smelled like some animal had died in there.

Mrs. Chin rolled the gas-powered push mower outside. For some reason, I had foolishly believed that the school might have had a ride-on since it was one heck of a big piece of property. But no such luck.

She found a gas can and filled the tank. "Here," Mrs. Chin said, putting one leg on the mower and tugging a few trial pulls on the cord. "I show you how to start it."

After about ten pulls, it started. The tiny muffler was rusted away and the engine roared like a wild animal. Mrs. Chin smiled at me and then turned and walked back into the house. I hadn't mowed a lawn in several years. I pushed the machine around to the front of the building and started cutting the grass. The noise of the mower drowned out everything, even the usual chorus of unhappy voices arguing in my head.

Chapter Fourteen

I know that the word, "haunted," is usually associated with ghosts, and some did say that the old building we lived in had ghosts. Stories circulated about murders and suicides that had taken place in this once grand old mansion, but I assumed these were more fictional than real. Nonetheless, few of us ventured down into the basement where the old furnace roared and rattled. There was a lot of old junk down there and it was dark and damp. If there were ghosts about the place, this was where they resided.

As for myself, I had never felt the presence of anything out of the ordinary in our home away from home. Yet I had this feeling that the building was "haunted" by something else. The walls, I am sure, had absorbed the anxiety, the grief, the despair, and the unceasing confusion and anger many of us carried around in our daily lives. You could not put this many whacked-out young people together under one roof and expect the architecture to remain unaffected. So, when chips of plaster fell from the ceiling in the middle of math class, maybe it wasn't just because the plaster was old and dry.

When glass windowpanes cracked the very instant Giselle read an e-mail from her boyfriend saying that he was dumping her for a new, more attractive girl back at her old high school, that was not sheer coincidence.

Fin, while trying to wire up some new speakers to his computer, discovered a kind of black mold growing on the wall behind the desks. He showed it to me and I thought it was disgusting. But Fin said, "I like it. Can we keep it?" Maybe he had somehow conjured it into existence. I was probably allergic to it, but I could see that Fin saw the mildew as a kind of pet and I couldn't break his heart.

"Fin, you are the strangest person I ever met," I said without a trace of insult in my voice.

"Thanks," he said.

There were many plumbing problems in the house. The girls complained long and often about this. Dribbly showers, taps that would not shut off, rusty water. Cromwell promised to fix everything but plumbers didn't come cheap. Mrs. Chin fixed her own plumbing problems in the kitchen with the help of her young refugee nephew who did the work free of charge. I'd walked in once on Cromwell himself in the boys' bathroom trying to fix a leak in the drain under a sink. He sounded like a man preparing to do battle with a dragon and his only weapons were a monkey wrench and a great vocabulary of curse words.

Some of my peers voiced fears that the house would actually collapse upon us one day, burying us all in one fell swoop (or one fallen roof) like in that story by Edgar Allan Poe. And if that were to happen, we'd spare the world our impending emergence back into mainstream society. I had dreams about just that. All of us under a pile of rubble. It was not such an unhappy thought. A mini-version of TEOTWAWKI, although it would be a great disappointment to those hopeful of even greater calamity. If demise was the name of the game, Fin said he would definitely prefer some kind of explosion. Possibly the furnace blowing up or, better yet, a crashing 747 with terrorists at the helm.

With the whole edifice in such a state of disrepair, what exactly was keeping the dilapidated building intact? Some kind of mental force field created by Dr. Cromwell was my theory.

The following week, Marsha Jordan (Marsbar to those of us who knew and loathed her) and Brian Fink disappeared. I don't mean they vanished. They were pulled from the school by their parents. It was not clear whether these had been paying parents or deadbeat parents. But it was a signal to us that things were only getting worse for FOA despite the upbeat pep talks given at least once a day by our headmaster. During those speeches, Cromwell always wore an academic black robe and one of those silly, flat graduation caps with a tassel hanging down in his face. The first time I had seen him do this was when I first arrived; I assumed he was simply and purely insane. He was a lunatic posing as a headmaster.

But somehow we all grew to accept his eccentricities. Although he was in charge, although he had a grand plan for improving society by sheltering and teaching even the dregs (the rich dregs), and despite the fact he had multiple degrees from respectable institutions (including Oxford University) on his office walls, some of us had a sneaking suspicion that he was just a grown-up version of one of us. Where were his wife and his two point five children, I would ask you.

Nowhere to be seen, that's where. This ratty old campus was his life. This pitiful assembly of young dullards and dimwits and demented teens was his family and his life. It was enough to make a young man like myself take pity, and I generally had pity for no one but myself. And that self-pity, along with my generic abhorrence of humankind and a finely cultivated self-loathing, was what I was all about.

• • •

Twice, Christine was not at her trailer when I went to visit her. The door was unlocked and I had even gone in once—not sure why—and called her name, looked in the rooms. Expecting what? I don't know. I was just checking to see that she was okay. The trailer had an odd abandoned feel to it although it was still cluttered with a lot of Christine's things. After that I had walked around downtown and gone to the wharf to give my regards to the swaying kelp and rockweed below. I studied the pull and tug of clear water and the gulls that sat upon the skin of the harbor water like toys, blinking at me in the afternoon springtime sunlight. I also rather admired the shiny, small black shells of the mussels that clung to the creosote posts that held up the wharf.

I didn't admire the local hoodlums in bomber jackets who smoked cigarettes and watched me sometimes as if they were plotting some evil thing to do to me when I wasn't looking. I didn't like the way they smoked or practiced long-distance spitting as if it were an Olympic event. Once, walking past them, I heard one hayseed refer to me as "retarded," which struck me as a peculiar misdiagnosis. *If I'm retarded, then what are you*? I wanted to say. But I didn't. I walked on by. I thought of the old connotation of the word "retarded" and the new. One of the lads let fly a grand bolus of spittle in my direction as I passed, and it fell short of the mark, although I didn't turn around to evaluate its quality or proximity.

I was thinking just then about the T.S. Eliot poem the ever-optimistic and loyal Professor Dodd had tried to shove down our throats. "I should have been a pair of ragged claws" or something . . . "scuttling across the floors of silent seas." From my perch on the end of the wharf, I had also often admired those scuttlers of the harbor, the lonely, graceful crabs angling along the bottom, shells on the outside (for good reason) and unaware of complications and dangers from the hazardous world above the waterline.

To get away from the depressing aura of the school, I made forays into town whenever I could. I kept expecting to run into Christine panhandling for change on the street, but she was nowhere to be seen. Each time I walked the tree-lined streets of the well-to-do Harborville citizens on my way back to Farnsworth, I secretly feared for her well-being and deep down longed for her company.

• • •

It was a warm Friday afternoon when, much to my surprise, *she* came looking for *me*. Classes were over and I was cleaning up the old flower beds in the front yard. All of my fellow students thought I'd been brainwashed into doing yard work. They really did. Ryan took great pleasure in making fun of me and saying things like, "Watch out. Who's gonna be next? You, Giselle? Suddenly you wake up one morning with a craving to wash dishes or shampoo the carpets?"

I was working on my exoskeleton, however. Like the scuttling crab, I had my defences in place for some things. Predators like Code-X, well above my waterline, didn't really pose much of a threat. All my really potent enemies were within.

But I admit it must have looked odd. The perfect young misanthrope giving up on a good afternoon back in his room glowering at the world in favor of kneeling down in a flower bed, rooting out old garbage and moldering leaves. I was filling great big, black garbage bags, some with trash, and some with leaves. I had even begun a compost pile out back behind the garage. Up until a week ago, I had never even known what compost was.

Once my hands were down in the rich, dark soil underneath, I found myself scooping it up and looking at its mystery. From inside the school, anyone looking out would clearly have assumed I had lost whatever was left of my mind. But I enjoyed the feel of the earth. I had added it to my small but growing list of things I approved of in this world.

I don't know how long she had been standing there but I felt her presence before I even looked up.

I let out a sigh. "I've been worried about you," I said.

There was an air of total defeat about her. She didn't speak.

"I don't know what to do," she said. "I don't know who to turn to."

I brushed the dirt off my hands and stood up. I had been truly relieved to see her, but suddenly, looking at the pain in her face, I wished she hadn't shown up. I'd been feeling strangely relaxed and now she had intruded. She might have read this in my face because she started to turn away.

"Wait," I said, putting my dirty hand on her flannel shirt. "What is it?"

"The landlord wants me out of the trailer. My mom said we had it for a couple more months, but not according to him. He says he has an eviction notice. The rent hasn't been paid, he says. I haven't been staying around there in the days because someone told me that the notice has to be delivered to me in person. I have to be there. If I'm not there when it's delivered, he can't kick me out."

"What are you going to do?"

"I don't know."

I reached out and touched her hair. It was long, dark, and tangled with only a tinge of fading red left in it. She hadn't taken care of it. She hadn't taken care of herself and she was wearing the same faded jeans and flannel shirt I'd seen her in several times before. I remembered that image of her asking people for money on the street. I remembered how she'd wolfed down the food in Alfredo's.

"Come on," I said. "I want to introduce you to Mrs. Chin."

I took her hand and led her around to the back of the school and into the kitchen. Mrs. Chin was washing massive metal pots. I remembered how Dr. Cromwell had once given curious little lectures that were supposed to inspire us to help with the housework. I think there may have been a bit of subliminal suggestion involved even. But the efforts must have failed. His mind control plan for household chores had clearly not kicked in yet.

Mrs. Chin bowed slightly as I introduced Christine, who was more than a little uncomfortable in this unfamiliar setting.

"I was wondering . . ." I began, but Mrs. C. didn't let me finish. She grabbed my dirty hands and said, "You must wash first. Then eat."

I stood at the sink and scrubbed my dirty hands and then passed the soap to Christine. She rolled up her sleeves partway and I couldn't help but stare at the scars again. On both sides of her arms. I looked away.

I wasn't hungry but could not convince Mrs. Chin of that. Within seconds it seemed she had grabbed some already cooked food from the big stainless steel refrigerator and heated it in the microwave.

Before both of us were steaming plates of chicken, mashed potatoes, and Chinese vegetables. Christine started to eat and I just kind of played with my food.

Mrs. Chin was back at the sink scrubbing a pot and when she spoke she said the oddest thing. "So is this the girl who's going to be your wife?" she asked me.

Christine couldn't help but laugh, accidentally spitting mashed potatoes onto my shirt.

"I . . . uh . . . don't think either of us is ready to get married," I said.

"I was married when I was fourteen," Mrs. Chin said. "He was a good man, my husband. No other man was like him."

"What happened to him?" Christine asked.

"Killed. Land mines. We were going to visit my mother. Walking though a field. Everything looked perfectly fine."

"Oh, my God," Christine said.

"Mrs. Chin is from Vietnam," I said.

"It was during the war?"

"No," Mrs. Chin said. "After. That is part of the sad thing. The war was long over. But after he was gone, I had nothing. No reason to stay. I joined others in a boat. First there was a refugee camp in Thailand and then here."

"How did you get here?" I asked. It was odd that Mrs. Chin had never really told any of us her story. Why now?

"Dr. Cromwell sponsored me. He had money then."

So, once upon a time, Dr. C. had had plenty of cash. Maybe born rich, maybe savvy in the stock market. But then he got it in his head to start this school. He dug a money pit and started tossing in the gold.

"Do you have any children?" Christine asked.

"Not any more," she said. And after that we fell silent.

When she was finished, she grabbed the plates. "You two go play," she said as if we were two little children. I looked at Christine and she was smiling now. Really smiling. I had never seen this side of her. She had a glow about her and it couldn't have just been the food.

"Better than Alfredo's," she said.

"It's all about the ambience," I said.

She gave me a puzzled look. Me and my big words. "Thank you, Mrs. Chin."

"My pleasure," she said.

Christine started to walk away with me but then she stopped. She walked back to Mrs. Chin and gave her a hug that caught her totally off guard. It was as if no one had hugged her in a long while. Then Christine turned back to me with a devilishly delightful look in her eye. "Let's go," she said.

"Let's go where?" I asked.

"Let's go play," she said.

Chapter Fifteen

The town of Harborville is surrounded by orchards and fields where cattle and sheep graze. As previously noted, it's truly Farmer Clem country where men and women drive old pickup trucks side by side with the townies in their silver SUVs. But it's also a fishing community, even though they say there aren't as many fish as there used to be. (We're a stubborn, thick-headed species and when it is obvious that we've performed some heinous blunder like nearly wiping out all the fish that once fed us, instead of easing up, we keep fishing until all the fish have disappeared.)

Because of the long funnel shape of the bay leading to the harbor, the tides vary dramatically. It takes roughly six hours to go from high tide to low and vice versa. I once heard an old guy on the wharf refer to the time when the tide is high or low as "slack water," meaning that at that particular time, it is not going up or down. If you were a Harborvillain with a boat, all of this tide business would be of some serious importance to you. At high tide, your Cape Islander could be boarded by simply stepping from the dock onto the deck. At a lower tide, you'd have to climb down the ladder. And at dead low tide, your pride and joy would be sitting flat on the stony bottom with little or no water under it at all and you wouldn't be going anywhere to fish.

And at that same low tide, when I would occasionally walk to the wharf to stare at the sea life below, I'd be out of luck. The sea foliage would be a lifeless looking mat of stuff on the sea floor, and the crabs and fish were somewhere else waiting to roll back in with the incoming tide, I suppose.

Not far from town, however, the retreating tides would leave great sloping banks of reddish mud that glistened in the sunlight like fresh paint. Christine led me away from Farnsworth and down through a field of grass, past some dewy-eyed cattle munching from the green shoots of grass. We climbed a couple of wooden fences and followed a narrow path through a maple and birch forest until we came to the edge of the harbor at a place far from town. We were all alone. The sky was robin's egg blue and there was absolutely no one around. We seemed completely cut off from the rest of the world.

Christine held her hand out to the vista of marsh grass and acre upon acre of fresh mud. "*Voilà*," she said. She was smiling now like I'd never really seen her smile before. And it was infectious. This crazy girl had me smiling now simply because I was looking at a whole lot of fresh, red mud.

We walked to the edge of the high waterline and stared down the steep slope of shining mud. At the bottom was a mere trickle of a little brook running towards the sea. It was hard to believe that six hours from now, the water would have returned and would be lapping at our feet if we were still standing here.

"It's the moon, right?" she asked. "The moon somehow controls the tides. But I don't really understand it."

"The moon is circling the earth, right? When the moon is closest to where we are, then the tide is high. So right now, it's the opposite. The moon is closest right now to . . . um . . . China or India or somewhere over there. It's on the other side of the earth, so all the water in the world is pulled in that direction."

"Wow. Mr. Science."

"Yeah, once upon a time, I had a thing for science, especially oceans and sea stuff."

"Great," she said, almost giggling now. I had never seen her like this. "Let's do a little experiment."

With that, she jumped off the edge and landed on her ass on the steep, muddy slope. She let out a yelp as she slid down the slippery side towards the bottom at breakneck speed, laughing the whole way down. It was like sliding down a hill on a sled. Only it wasn't winter, there was no snow and no sled. Just a bright reddish incline of wet mud.

At the bottom she came to a stop, splashing her feet in the shallow water. "Now it's your turn," she yelled up to me. Her clothes were covered with the muck and she had put her muddy hands up to her face which was now imprinted with two hand prints of red.

I stared at her. "No way," I said.

"Please?" she asked.

"You want me to jump?" I asked. I think I wanted to do it just then. I really did. But something inside me was holding back. I couldn't let go. I just couldn't do it. I shook my head. "You're crazy, you know that, don't ya?"

With that, she got up onto her feet and began to climb on all fours up the slippery side, getting more covered with bright red mud with each effort. She was panting when she got to the top.

"You want to do it, don't you? I can tell."

"I don't know," I said. "It just seems nuts. Look at you."

She caught me off guard. I was confused and feeling light-headed and then she took my face in her muddy hands and she kissed me on the mouth. I can still remember the taste of the mud and the surprise feeling of the small metal stud in the middle of her tongue..

And it tasted wonderful.

"Are you ready?" she asked.

"Sure," I said, finally convinced.

And together we leaped from the grassy edge, landed with a splat and began to toboggan ourselves towards the bottom, screaming the whole way. When we got to the little stream at the bottom, my head was swirling and the gulls above were laughing at us. We were both breathing hard as she kissed me a second time. Never before in my life had I felt so wild and free.

"Let's do it again," I said.

"Bet I can beat you to the top."

"Bet you can't."

We both began scrambling and, about halfway up, when she got ahead of me, I tugged at her leg. I did it in a playful way and, as she slipped back towards me, she turned over and pulled me down onto her. I lost my footing and we began sliding ever so slowly back towards the bottom of the empty harbor. I had never held my body close to a girl before. It felt great. She was laughing and so was I. I clawed at the mud to slow our descent. I didn't want the moment to end. Her shirt sleeves were unbuttoned now and I couldn't help but notice those marks on her arms again. I knew that there was something about this girl that was both worrisome and maybe even dangerous. But I would choose to ignore it. I kissed her again and she liked it. I could feel the heat of her and the shape of her beneath me.

When we came to rest at the bottom again, I looked directly into her eyes. There was no fear or hurt there now. Only the reflection of my own muddy face and the blue sky above.

"Are you okay?" I asked, not wanting to end this but not wanting her to think I was a total pervert.

"Let's stay like this forever," she said and I felt the hair on the back of my neck stand on end.

"Forever," I echoed. And we lay like that for a very long while listening to the sound of each other breathing.

• • •

But the moon was circling the planet. It was saying goodbye to India and China. The tide began to rise ever so slowly. At some point, I knew that *forever* would have to end. Without saying a word, I stood up, took Christine's hand, and we climbed the difficult embankment together. But as soon as we reached the top, she leaped again—high into the air and landing further down on the slope. I followed her lead and leaped as high into the air as I could. For a split second, I almost felt like I could fly. I came down hard and fast but it didn't hurt at all as I landed on the steep but soft angle and began to skid downward towards Christine below me. This time I grabbed her playfully and we wrestled in the mud, rolling around until she was on top of me this time and I was pinned beneath her.

I pushed her off and then pounced. We were two wild animals at play, both of us totally covered in bright red mud. Our feet were in the rising water now and we eventually clambered up the muddy slope for the final time.

At the top, we looked at each other and couldn't believe our eyes. We looked outrageous. "What will we do now?"

"Come back to my place," she said. "We'll try to get cleaned up."

• • •

If the Harborvillains had seen anything like us before, they weren't letting on. They stared and some laughed. "Pretend everything is normal," she said, holding her head up high.

"I can't stand it when people stare at me," I said, and glared back at one particularly sour old woman who was clutching her purse and scowling at us.

The mud was starting to dry now and felt truly strange on my skin. I could scrape off little chips of it from the back of my hands, so I flicked some in her direction and the lady turned and walked away.

Christine's neighbors on Sneezy Lane gave us some hard looks and it seemed odd that no one was laughing at us. Just about everyone we'd encountered had looked at us as if we'd committed a crime.

Christine invited me in. "Take a shower. You go first and then me."

I'm pretty sure that she meant just that. I would take a shower, find some clothes that I could wear, and head back to Farnsworth. But the whole afternoon had been such a wild ride. I had never experienced the flood of emotions that were sweeping through me. It was like I had shed a skin. Here beneath my new mud hide, I was a different person. And I was feeling a weird natural high. But at the same time it was all kind of scary. I wasn't sure I was ready to be naked in this crazy, wonderful girl's house.

"I'll clean up back at school," I said. I brushed the dry mud from her lips and some from her cheek and I kissed her like I really knew how to kiss. I was both thrilled and shocked to discover that there was no special trick or skill to kissing. It was a thing that came most naturally.

"See you tomorrow," I said. "And thanks. Thanks for . . ." I was at a loss for words, so I pointed at my muddy self. "Thanks for this. I mean it."

$\bullet \quad \bullet \quad \bullet$

Walking back through town, even though I was on my own now, I felt brazen. I ignored the looks or I looked right back at people and nodded a hello as if nothing about me was out of the norm. The mud was like a uniform and I wore it proudly. I almost wished that I didn't have to wash it off.

I walked up the driveway of Farnsworth Academy and wondered what the other students would think when they saw me. I noticed how much better the lawns looked and that the flowers were blooming now: daffodils and crocuses. Just as I was about to grab the door handle to the front door, it opened. And there stood Cromwell. At first, there was a look of shock, of disbelief. I don't even think he knew who or what he was looking at. The mud was dry now, kind of caked and cracking all over me, even on parts of my face.

I didn't say a word. The shock gave way to something else. Cromwell's facial features softened and then he was smiling at me. It was a big shit-eating smile like I had never seen on him before.

Chapter Sixteen

Dr. Cromwell said nothing at all to me. He just held open the door and let me walk through. Some of the other kids were lounging around downstairs and one of the guys said, "What happened to you, man?" but I didn't answer. Fin blinked hard when I walked into the room but, being Fin, he didn't bother to ask for a story. And what a story it was.

I took a shower, and as I watched the red muddy water pool at my feet and swirl into the drain below, I went through a range of emotions. At first I was still holding onto the glow but as the mud washed off beneath the lukewarm shower water, I felt something different. Loss. I wondered if I would ever feel that good again. I didn't trust feeling happy. Other kids must have spent big ragged-ass chunks of their lives being happy from time to time but not me. I washed my hair and I scrubbed out the mud from under my fingernails and when I walked back to my room with just a towel around my waist, I felt not like "a new man" at all, but I felt changed.

I could see before me the easy path headed back to the way I used to be, but I also had this new belief that I could choose another route. A more complicated one. I understood that I had now been given permission to stop hating the world. I could do this if I wanted to. It was all up to me.

I tossed my dirty clothes into a black plastic garbage bag, sealed it and walked it downstairs where I put it with a pile of trash to go out from the kitchen. I had the desperate hope that it wasn't the last time I'd come home with clothes I'd have to throw away. I would have loved to call Christine but her phone had been disconnected long ago. No phone, no computer, no e-mail. She was living in her own little lost world. I desperately needed to talk to someone.

So I talked to Fin. I explained what happened that afternoon.

"Man, she sounds deranged," was all he said. "I'd steer clear of her."

"You don't get it. She's the best thing that ever happened to me. Today was amazing."

Fin looked at me with a kind of sad disappointment in his eyes. I was moving away from being his friend is what he was thinking. I could tell. I was a traitor to our death-rattle alliance. He turned back to his computer and began to punch in keys.

I tried to re-establish our old reality. "Don't worry, dude. If I'm feeling this buzzed today, it's pretty certain that tomorrow our solar system will be sucked into a black hole. I can feel it coming. All matter will collapse in on itself and it'll be the end of the world as we know it."

Without turning around, Fin shot back one of his old standbys: "No more homework."

As if we ever did much homework at FOA. It was challenge

enough to get students to come to class. Even harder to keep them awake. Harder still to get anyone to read a textbook or even a magazine. In English, Mr. Dodd, who seemed a whole lot less passionate about literature or his students' education as the financial crisis developed—well, he resorted to buying us all comic book versions of classic books: *Moby-Dick*, *Great Expectations*, and *Gulliver's Travels*.

• • •

In the morning, my muddy clothes appeared mysteriously returned in a neat little plastic package hanging from my door: shirt, jeans, underwear, socks—all perfectly clean and neatly folded. At breakfast I asked Mrs. Chin if she had done this.

"If a boy rolls in mud, you wash up things afterwards. You don't throw them away. Cleanliness is next to godliness." Her face was stern and some of the other kids, of that rare breed of FOA students who actually showed up for breakfast, laughed out loud at her.

"Thanks, Mrs. Chin. I really appreciate it."

"No harm done," was all she said, not letting down the serious demeanor.

• • •

I still had a little buzz going in the back of my brain: sunlight, Christine, slaloming down the bright mud, and ultimately the feel of her body against mine. It was going to be hard to stay focused in math class with the frizzy-haired mom of a former FOA student who was "filling in." She was well intended but hadn't had a lot of practice baby-sitting a class full of bored, spoiled teenagers from mostly broken homes. She didn't stand a chance but nobly put a good face on each day's disastrous class. Oddly enough, it was Code-X who was the most attentive student and raised his hand to ask random mathematical questions totally unrelated to the day's lesson (if you could call it that). His favorite topic was exponential growth and mathematical pyramid structures. I'm sure it was all related to money. Despite the evidence, Code-X (now referred to as Kotex by those who were not in his fan club—and there were many) truly believed that happiness was to be achieved by amassing wealth by any means necessary. This was, I suppose, the code of Code-X.

So I decided I would skip Frizzy-Mom's Math, and the video Dodd was going to show: Mel Gibson in *Macbeth* filmed on location in Scotland. I might make it back for history, but if not, I'd be there for Doc's afternoon "seminar" on weighty issues. Today he was to continue lecturing on "Social Development," an issue that many of us felt was irrelevant. Doc never implied that any of his psychology textbook talk was about any of us. But he hoped we would draw some conclusions with our own gray matter on the various sub-headers for development like "Emotions, Personality Development, Interpersonal Relationships, and Morality."

I decided that it hadn't been very respectful to cut classes without telling Cromwell I was doing it. So I knocked on his office door. Maybe this was part of the new me.

"Come in." He was on the phone but, when he saw me, he put his caller on hold.

"I'm going to miss a couple of classes this morning," I said. I had never once told him before when I was leaving the school grounds. Few of us did even though there were rules in a handbook given out to parents that said this was mandatory. There were many things that were "mandatory" at Farnsworth that no one paid attention to. This, I think, was part of our preparation for the so-called real world that we would enter once we "graduated" from the academy of failed humans.

"And?" he asked politely.

"I'd like to bring back a friend for a visit. Is that permissible?"

Doc scratched his head. "I would think a visit would be just fine. Is it an old friend?

"No, someone new. A girl from town. I like her a lot." I was surprised at myself for volunteering that final bit of information.

"We would be pleased to have your friend come as a guest," he said in a most formal manner.

"Thanks."

• • •

As I walked down the school driveway, I noticed a flower bed that needed weeding and I studied some of the ragged bushes, wondering if there were tools in the garage for trimming them. I wanted the yard to look shipshape when the black hole arrived to swallow us all.

I knocked at Christine's rattly door several times but got no answer. Then I remembered about the landlord. Christine wasn't answering her door. I yelled out her name and still didn't get any response. I tried opening the door and could get it open a crack but it was held there by one of those little chain locks. I yelled for her again and I heard a voice.

"It's me. Carson. Can you open up?"

"Wait," she said groggily.

I waited.

She arrived in an old frayed housecoat a couple of sizes too big. Her hair was a mess and she seemed not at all thrilled to see me. She'd still been asleep.

"Got any coffee?" I asked.

She undid the chain and let me in. She wasn't talking and she seemed like she wasn't at all happy to see me. It was like yesterday had never happened.

She pointed to a kettle and a jar of Maxwell Instant. "There's no milk," she said.

"Black is okay. Any sugar?"

She pointed to a shelf above and I reached for a bag that was hard.

"Perfect," I said, putting water in the kettle and plugging it in.

Christine just looked at me.

"I'd like you to come visit the school today," I said. "I got permission from the headmaster. He said it was okay."

"Why?" she asked.

That was a tough one to answer. If I had lived in some kind of normal world, if this had been a TV show or a story in a book, I might have said something like, "So I can introduce you to my friends." But I didn't really think of my classmates as friends. I was even having my doubts about Fin, although I knew he was just acting a little cranky because he felt I was abandoning him. I threw my hands up in the air. "I just wanted to," I said. "Will ya?"

Christine didn't know. The no-answer answer lasted until the kettle whistled and I made for myself one of the worst cups of coffee I would ever drink. I handed her a cup of the dark, toxic liquid and she took a cautious sip. If there was some world's record for awkward silence, we would have been in the Guinness book. Had it been an Olympic event, we would have blown away all the competition. It stretched out nicely as I stared into the dark, hot pool. It wasn't until I stirred my coffee with my finger and then sucked on it that she looked up.

"Okay," she said.

It seemed to take forever for her to get dressed and get ready to go with me. I picked up a couple of movie star magazines and the book Mel had given her. I coached myself not to rush her. It was one hell of a way to spend the morning.

When she finally emerged from her bedroom, she looked different. Her hair was fixed and she had on a blouse and skirt. The thing that drew my attention right away was the blouse. It only covered her arms to her elbows. The scars were visible on both arms. I had a hard time pretending not to notice. "How's this look?" she asked timidly.

I was afraid to suggest she put on something with long sleeves so people wouldn't notice. But I knew if I said anything wrong, she'd never come. "That's perfect," I said, flipping open one of those teen girl magazines. "You look just like the girls in here."

• • •

To say she was a little self-conscious is an understatement. Right off the bat, two workmen sitting in a pickup truck right on the street stared at her as we walked by. They just sat there in their damn truck and leered at her and they didn't care who saw. I felt like kicking that truck or walking up to the men and telling them off. But it was a delicate balance here. It was like Christine and I were on some kind of tightrope. Maybe I could figure out a way to locate that truck later and do some damage to it. Puncture the tires, maybe, or put sugar in the gas tank.

But right now, I was trying to stay focused. Christine seemed very fragile. She wasn't the girl from yesterday at all. I wasn't even sure why I was doing this.

As we walked through downtown on our way, Mel was just opening his store and he waved. Someone was washing the front windows of Alfredo's and there was a dog tethered to a post outside the drugstore wagging its tail as he waited for his owner's return. A couple of hayseeds were pumping gas into their tractor and a mailman was delivering mail through the slots in the doors on Main Street. It all seemed like the most ordinary day imaginable. We walked silently through the town, having brought the awkward silence along as some kind of unwanted luggage. Finally, I asked her how she was feeling.

"Fine," she said. "I feel just fine.

Chapter Seventeen

There was the sound of worlds colliding.

I'd like to be able to say that my fellow Flunkoutonians made Christine's visit easy but they did not. But you have to remember that the sum total social skills of all thirty-some of my classmates was probably equivalent to the social skills of one adolescent mollusc. Whatever was the nature of our diverse upbringings, we had arrived at a point in our lives where we felt successful if we could get out of bed in the morning, put on clothes, and stumble downstairs. Getting through a day without getting angry or inadvertently insulting a fellow human being was worthy of a medal.

Everyone was gathered in the dilapidated library, draped over old chairs or lounging by the windows or simply sitting on the floors. We walked into the room and sat towards the back on an old desk that may once have been owned by the wealthy man who had built this now-decomposing estate. Giselle and Mary looked at Christine, did a quick inventory of the way she looked, and shook their heads and clucked their tongues. Ryan and Patrick looked at me and winked. A few other heads turned our way.

Christine whispered in my ear, "Why are they looking at me like that?"

I whispered back, "Because they're idiots. Don't pay them any attention. Just relax."

Balled gum wrappers were flicked across the room but not at us. Someone farted and boys laughed. A girl's voice offered a review of the fart: "Gross." A guy's voice wondered if there was a dead animal in here. Someone turned their MP3 player up so loud it could be heard across the room.

Giselle and Mary were staring at Christine now openly. They were staring at her arms and when Christine realized this, she folded her arms and leaned into me. I gave the two staring girls the finger and a truly venomous look until they looked away.

And then Dr. C. walked in, dignified, head held high, that intriguing look of slightly crazed intelligence on his face. He was wearing his black robe as was the norm for the scheduled "seminar." I could tell from the look on Christine's face that she was a little freaked.

"Don't worry," I said to her in a hushed voice, "it's just this little theatrical thing he does to get our attention. He's not going to sacrifice a goat or anything."

"What about virgins? Is he going to sacrifice virgins?"

"You think he'd find any in this room?"

Christine smiled and gave me an elbow in the ribs.

Despite what most students would tell you to your face, most of them liked and even, dare I use the word, respected Dr. Cromwell. He was paternal and he was unique. And he had taken us all into his last-chance educational institution when all else had failed. His methods, if anyone could call them methods, were both eccentric and erratic. His goal, as stated in the glossy but misleading brochure, was to "inspire, educate, and prepare the leaders of tomorrow." I doubt, however, that many parents had bought into that bullshit. I'm not even sure Dr. Chromewall had very high aspirations for any of us. I think his plan was simple: provide a reasonably safe and emotionally stable haven for miscreants, keep them alive as best one could, and turn them back out into the world when they are of legal age to fend for themselves. Which I guess you could call. "Inspire, educate, and prepare" (IEP), but as to the "leader" aspect? Nah.

Cromwell stood at a small wooden podium arranging his notes, as if he were about to address the student body of Harvard. The little black tassel hung down the front of his graduation style board hat. It was a slightly preposterous scene but we had all laughed at him before and he had not acknowledged or even seemed to notice our ignorance. So we did not laugh at him any more.

Dr. C.'s lectures were all of a psychological nature and, for the most part, they were well over our heads, but most of us tended to listen anyway. Often what he had to say rang true about me or about the students I knew. In the deep reaches of my mind, it had even occurred to me more than once that maybe I would someday become a psychiatrist for a living. (I would need a job some day, after all, wouldn't I, if the world did not end?) If push came to shove, I'm sure I'd rather work with crazy people than with the so-called normal ones.

"Last week, as you'll recall, we summed up Eriksson's theory of personality and identity development. Today I'd like to begin by touching on James Marcia's four kinds of identities."

Christine squeezed my arm gently and looked puzzled. I nodded reassuringly.

"Dr. Marcia identified the four identities as identity achievement, foreclosure, identity diffusion, and moratorium." There were a couple of yawns in the crowd. Cromwell stopped, looked around, cleared his throat, and continued. "If you are secure in who you are, you have reached identity achievement. If you are having what some might call an identity crisis, your identity is in moratorium. If you simply buy into someone else's rules or way of looking at the world, you have identity foreclosure, and if you have no real direction in your life, you are experiencing identity diffusion."

Leave it to Ryan to raise his hand and play the smart-ass card. "What if you experience all of those things at once?"

Cromwell seemed to take the question seriously but answered, "Then your name is Ryan Luger."

A few chuckles. Ryan was pleased that he had drawn attention to himself as usual. "My friends call me Code-X."

"Kotex, you mean," Patrick added.

"Shut up, asswipe," the Code responded.

Cromwell put up a hand, which made him look like some holy man blessing the masses. The group quieted down. "Dr. Marcia later took a hard look at his own theories. It was during the Vietnam War and he saw thousands of people protesting and it occurred to him there must be a fifth type of identity." He paused for dramatic effect. "Anyone like to guess what that fifth identify type is?"

"The hippie?" Ryan shouted out, lifting a two-fingered V of a peace sign up into the air.

Cromwell smiled. "Marcia called this type alienated achievement, meaning that you have looked around at your society and decided you want no part of it. In effect, you decide to separate yourself from the society you live in and that becomes a big part of who you are."

I know I was not alone with what I was feeling just then, because the room had fallen silent. I hated it when labels had been put on me down through the years at school, and there had been many. The counsellors and the shrinks had come up with a sizeable list but they had all been names for *what was wrong with me*. This was different. Maybe I was an alienated achiever. I defined who I was by what I was not.

Christine squirmed noticeably. I touched her arm and she jumped slightly. "Don't worry," I whispered. "Cromwell knows we all have a five-minute attention span. He won't be long."

Dr. C. told a story about an old chum of his from university, an alienated achiever who went on to volunteer in AIDS orphanages in South Africa. He followed that with some thoughts on self-understanding and self-esteem and did his usual in conclusion: a very lame joke.

"Guy goes in to his psychiatrist and says, 'Doc, I keep having these camping dreams and in the dream, I'm not *in* the tent, I *am* the tent. Sometimes I'm this big military style tent and other times I'm this little pup tent.'" Pause. "The psychiatrist thinks for a minute and then tells the man, `I know what your problem is. 'You're just two tents.'"

Groans all around.

Dr. Cromwell tipped his scholar's hat to us and, as if on cue, Mrs. Chin opened the doors and rolled in a big cart with several pizzas and large bottles of Pepsi, Coke, and Seven-Up. This was the way a typical seminar ended. Everybody got up and started grabbing for pizza slices like they hadn't eaten in a week. I left Christine and went to fight for my share. "Sit tight."

When I returned, two-fisted with pepperoni pizza wedges, Dr. Cromwell was walking towards us. He held out his hand and Christine reluctantly shook it. Cromwell nodded at the animals. "Textbook Pavlovian response," he said.

Cromwell noticed her arms right away. But he quickly looked up and into her eyes. "Nice to have you come for a visit."

"I enjoyed your talk," she said rather nervously.

Cromwell smiled. "I'm glad someone appreciated it," he said in the gentlest of tones imaginable and then his eyes drifted towards the kitchen. "I must get in there before it's all gone." He turned and went for pizza.

I gave Christine a tour of the school and she pretended to be interested, but I could tell she was uncomfortable. Finally, I led her back to the kitchen where Mrs. Chin was putting things away. There was a considerable amount of noise involving banging pots around. Mrs. Chin said hello and then more or less ignored us. I knew we'd be more comfortable here.

"Why did you bring me to the school?" Christine asked.

"I don't really know. It's just that, well, I wanted you to see a bit of what my life is all about." It sounded really lame now that I said it out loud.

"My school was never like this."

"How come you dropped out?"

"I didn't really ever drop out. I just couldn't handle it anymore. I couldn't stand what people said about me. The longer I stayed there the more I hated myself. Because I believed they were right."

"What did they say?"

She shook her head. "It doesn't matter." There was an air of defeat about her.

"I think you're wonderful," I said. I had rehearsed those words in my head for just this occasion.

She blushed and lowered her head.

Then she began to cry.

Chapter Eighteen

Christine insisted that she walk home alone. "This has been great. I just need some time to walk by myself and think. I'll be okay. You should . . . study."

"Not too many of us actually study. Dr. Cromwell doesn't believe in tests."

"How do you know how you are doing?"

I shrugged. "You just know." I had a hard time explaining the school's educational philosophy, although I am sure Doc had one. "I guess they figure that if we show up for class and if we learn, well . . . anything, that's a good thing. Like I explained to you before, most of us here have been written off by the traditional school system."

"Carson," she said. "You're not the loser you think you are."

Maybe I was the one who blushed just then. "That's about the nicest thing anyone has ever said to me. You sure I can't walk you home?"

"No. I just need some time to myself."

"But you're okay?"

"Yeah. Very okay."

I opened the front door and she walked out. She didn't look back and I had this chill run down my spine. I suddenly realized how much this girl meant to me. I had never had a girlfriend before. Had I actually fallen for Christine? I didn't even have any reference points. It was downright scary. She and I were from different worlds and I didn't really care about that. Just watching her walk out the driveway, I felt this great sorrow inside me. Right then it didn't seem to matter that I would certainly be able to see her tomorrow. Right now she wasn't here with me and that hurt more than anything in the world.

What if this was what falling in love was all about? One minute you feel overjoyed, ecstatic, and then—*boom*—the next, as she walks away, you feel alone and broken. I wasn't sure I was emotionally ready for this roller-coaster ride.

A kind of gloom settled over me as I closed the door and shuffled up the steps towards my room. Maybe I was better off with my former self—that nice, neat package of pessimism and anger. In that world I had created for myself, everything made a kind of sense. Whatever had happened to my motto about hating the world and everything in it? It simply no longer seemed to apply.

And the world was a much more confusing place and I was a much more confused pilgrim wandering in that world.

Dr. Cromwell was coming down as I was going up. The robe was gone. He was wearing a white shirt and black tie and faded jeans. He was worried about something.

"Nice speech," I said.

"Can we go outside, Carson? I want your opinion about those flowering bushes."

"The azaleas?" I asked. I had been trying to figure out the names for the different flowers and shrubs. I had gone so far as to look up "pruning azaleas" on the Internet. Weird, eh? Six months ago, the only thing I was looking up on the Net was information about neo-Nazis or chasing down conspiracy theories about chemicals being put in milk that would eventually turn us all into zombies. Now I actually knew how to prune flowering shrubs and when.

Cromwell took big strides as we walked across the lawn but he looked down the whole time as if watching out not to step on earthworms or ants. "I liked your friend," he said.

"She's kind of quiet," I said. Christine hadn't really spoken to anyone other than me and Mrs. Chin.

"She was the one with the mud, right?"

"Right. First she rolled in it, or I should say rolled *down* it, and then she convinced me to follow."

"Do you think that was wise?"

"Yes."

"Good." Doc wasn't really lecturing me here. This was just his typical way of testing my resolve about what I really felt. He even explained to me once what the technique was and it wasn't all that far from Pavlov's conditioning of dogs. It was only different in that he wasn't really trying to convince me of anything new. He wanted me to be convinced of what I myself was thinking. Let's call it "How to Take an Opinion or an Inclination and Turn it into an Attitude or a Belief."

"I couldn't help but notice her arms," he said, stopping right in front of that azalea bush that I had pruned a couple of days ago. He studied the tips where I had cut the gangly woody branches with the dull pruning shears.

"I think I cut the ends off at the wrong time of year. I didn't know that until afterwards. I hope I didn't kill it."

"It will recover," Dr. C. said. "Plants, like people, are resilient. How long have you known Christine?"

"Not long. Why?"

"Do you know if she's ever been institutionalized?"

"What?" I couldn't believe he was saying this.

"Maybe that was a bad way of saying it. It's just that I've seen this before. In my practice, before I started the school."

"Saw what?"

"Sometimes people, especially teenage girls, injure themselves on purpose. They do things . . ."

I looked away from him. "I don't think they're needle marks. I don't think she's doing drugs."

Doc remained calm. "I don't think she is either."

"I just figured it was some kind of childhood injury." I swallowed hard as I said this. "I don't know, something from a car accident."

"Could be. Anything is possible, but . . ."

"But what?" I was getting angry now. Why was he trying to ruin this one good thing in my life? Why would he do this to me?

Doc looked directly at me and I could only look down at the ground. "But like I said, I've seen something like this before. My guess is that the scars are left from something she did to herself."

"That's crazy!" I was shouting now. I could feel tears welling up in my eyes and they burned. I held back and sucked my lower lip.

"Carson, we all feel pain. We've all been hurt. Sometimes, when you are young, you are hurt so badly inside that you come to a point where you stop feeling anything."

"I know," I said. "I think I've been there."

And then he surprised me with what he said next. "And so have I. There are reasons why I took up the study of psychology and why I started this school. I'll tell you about them sometime."

"But Christine is like the best thing that ever happened to me. And now you're going to tell me that she's . . . ?" But I didn't even know how to finish the sentence.

"Let me finish. Suppose you numb yourself for so long that it scares you and you realize that you need to feel something. Happy, angry . . . anything. But it's just not there. So one day, you pick up something sharp—a pin, a nail, a pencil maybe—and you push it into your skin. Maybe you do it at first because you don't like yourself and you want to punish yourself. You feel pain. You don't exactly like it, but you realize that at least you are feeling something. At least you are still alive and this is what it takes to feel anything."

"But she wouldn't do that. She's smart. She's got a difficult life, but why would she try to injure herself?"

"Intelligence doesn't have anything to do with it."

"Why are you doing this to me?" I had snapped back to feeling angry at Cromwell. I was sure he had some adult ulterior motive to make sure that this problem girl, Christine, dropped out of my life.

Then he did something that really freaked me out.

He pulled his shirt out of his pants and lifted it up over his belly. I started to turn away but he made me look at him.

"See this," he said, drawing his finger over a long, pinkish scar across his stomach. "I did that with a broken Coke bottle when I was thirteen."

"You tried to kill yourself?"

"That's what the doctors asked me. Those exact words."

He dropped his shirt and looked suddenly somewhat embarrassed. "No, I told them that I didn't try to kill myself. But I didn't have any other explanation. And I didn't understand it myself. Years later, when I studied psychology at university and I myself was in therapy, it started to make sense. I was not so different from Christine."

"Maybe you're wrong about her."

"I don't think so."

"But I've never seen her try to harm herself."

"Could be that she stopped. But those arms. That's a lot of scarring. What are her parents like? Should I talk to them?"

I explained about Christine's living situation, but made Dr. C. promise not to turn her in to Social Services.

"What's your gut instinct, Carson? What should be done?"

My gut instinct was that if anyone tried too hard to do anything—to help, to advise, or anything at all—that she'd probably run. I think she was close to it when I first met her. If she ran, I was certain I'd never see her again. I decided to turn it around.

"Who are you trying to help?" I asked. "Her or me?"

Dr. Cromwell tucked his shirt back in. "I'm not really at all sure I can help either one of you."

"Don't give me that crap!" I suddenly screamed at him.

"If she has been so unhappy that she's driving nails into her arms, there must be something I can do." I said the word *I* with great emphasis.

"If she is prone to—I hate to use the word, but I want you to hear it—self-mutilation, then she could still be in serious trouble. That's why I asked if she'd been institutionalized. Not that I think much of those places. But I'd like to know if she's ever been properly treated."

"I think she's been to guidance counsellors, maybe social workers." But even as I said those words, it all seemed so hopeless. It suddenly sunk in deeply what Doc was saying. She was a very damaged young woman.

And I had let myself fall in love with her. Now it was me I was worried about. Why was that happening? I was worried about Christine, for sure, but I was also worrying about me. If she was that injured, then it was possible that it could never work out between us. One way or the other I would lose her. And my newfound sunny, muddy world would be drowned in a rising tide of despair. "God damn it!" I screeched out loud.

Cromwell stood still and looked up at the leaves of the big old oak above us.

"What can I do?" I finally asked. I was crying openly now, but I know these weren't tears of unhappiness. These were tears of rage.

"You want my advice as a professional or as a friend?"

"I don't know," I said.

"Do you want me to tell you what I think you should do if you were my son, then?"

"No."

"Then I'll give you my advice as a friend because I think you've already decided what to do."

"I know."

Chapter Nineteen

What I had decided to do about Christine was this: I would be there for her. What Doc had said about her scared me but it didn't scare me away. I knew I had to try to help her even though I wasn't sure how.

I went back to my room to think about it, to sleep on it. Fin was in a grouchy mood. He didn't like the new me. I could understand that. I wasn't sure who the new me was but I think I did like him better than the old me. Only it wasn't easy, this new role. Just when I had begun to feel lighter, now here I was feeling heavier. I felt responsible. I had to make sure Christine was going to be okay. And I had no idea how I would do this. I kept thinking about those scars on her arms. I kept hoping that Dr. Cromwell was dead wrong.

I had brought Christine further into my life by inviting her to the school. In a way, she had been brave to show up. Now I would go slowly. Not push it. Wait until tomorrow. Hell, she didn't have a phone so I couldn't call. No computer at her place so I couldn't send her a message. Just hang back and wait until tomorrow and then . . . maybe just be her friend.

• • •

The next day it rained buckets in the morning. It slowed by noon and, by the time I finished my last class, the skies had mostly emptied themselves. I borrowed some rain gear and set off for town under a constant drizzle from a low, bruised sky. Despite the gloom, the leaves on the trees glistened. Everything was green and alive.

Main Street was mostly empty and I moved away from the road when the SUVs roared by, slamming into potholes and sending volleys of water at mere pedestrians like me. I walked fast and discovered I was almost running. It could have been the weather or maybe something else, some inner nervousness that I was feeling. I began the long, uphill ascent of Clark Street to the trailer park.

At first, everything seemed perfectly normal. Cats running across the street, dogs barking. The usual rusted-out cars in all the right places. But then I turned onto Sneezy Lane, feeling the nervous thrill rising in me because I was about to see Christine again and . . .

It wasn't there.

Her trailer. Her home. It was gone.

I walked up to where it had been. The outline of bare earth surrounded by green grass. My first reaction was that it was like it had been beamed into space. Straight up. It seemed crazy. But then I saw the tracks, the ruts. Someone had backed a truck up and towed it away.

I looked up and saw that the power line had been disconnected and three loose wires hung from the pole. On the ground, I noticed the plumbing pipes that had been cut and capped. I tried to steady myself and sort it out. It was a trailer. There had been wheels under it. For some reason, someone came and moved it. Drove it away. It suddenly occurred to me that it might have happened when Christine was at Farnsworth. She would have come home to this. I swallowed hard as I felt cold fear sweep up the back of my scalp. Her home had been driven away. She would have seen this and . . . what?

She was already gone. I was certain I'd never see her again.

I banged loudly on one of the neighbor's doors. A young mother clutching a sleeping baby to her chest came to the door. The woman was smoking a cigarette and some of the ash had dropped onto the blanket of the sleeping baby. She looked at me with mistrust.

"Do you know where Christine went?" I pointed to the empty place where the trailer had been.

She didn't say anything at first, just eyed me suspiciously and took another drag on her cigarette. "Who?"

"Christine. She was living right there."

"Oh, yeah. Her. The girl. It's hard to say. Did she, like, owe you money or something? You seem upset."

"No, nothing like that. I'm her friend."

"You're the boyfriend?"

I didn't exactly know what this meant in the mind of this person. It sounded more like an accusation of something. "Something like that," I said, hoping it would lead to some answers.

Another drag from the cigarette. "Landlord must have just sold the rig. I don't think they even gave her time to pack her things up. Look."

Beside the big, green metal garbage dumpster were nearly a dozen boxes, some with clothes spilling out of them.

Christine's worldly possessions: boxed and left for the garbage. The rain had soaked everything thoroughly and some of the boxes were split and collapsing.

"Did you see her when she found out?"

"Yesterday afternoon. How could I miss it? She sat there crying in my front yard. I didn't know what to do. I had the baby and all."

In other words, she didn't want to get involved.

"Did you talk to her?"

"I thought about it but I didn't really know her. She kept to herself. I thought it best not to get involved. After a while she just walked away. Poor kid," she said finally, as if that summed it up and put an end to the story.

I walked over to the boxes by the dumpster hoping to find some clues. In one of the split boxes, I found an old school notebook with some pictures taped inside. The notebook was ruined. Everything was wet. There were only four pictures inside. One was of a little girl sitting on a pony at a fair. She was smiling and it looked like the happiest day of her life. Another was of the same little girl with two adults. Christine and her parents were sitting on a dock by a lake. They all had swimsuits on. Everything looked perfectly normal. The other two pictures were school photos, the sample ones with printing on them. Christine's parents had probably never bought the school pictures; this was all they had kept. She was older here: twelve in one, maybe fourteen in the other. The eyes had changed. At twelve her eyes sparkled in the photographer's lighting. By fourteen, there was something else: the seed of the hurt and fear that I had first seen in her.

I put the pictures carefully into my shirt pocket and headed back to town.

Clark Street is steep and I had never really noticed what it feels like in the back of your ankles to be walking down a steep slope. If you're used to doing all your walking on flat surfaces, these are muscles that don't get much use. I wouldn't exactly call it pain but something else. An odd sensation of tension. And it spread from there up my legs and through me. I felt as if I were about to explode.

• • •

I didn't know anywhere else to go, so I walked to the harbor and out onto the wharf. The usual trucks and men were parked there. The men had nothing better to do but to wait for the rising tide so they could head out onto the water and fish for whatever was left out there. One or two nodded at me as I walked by, another simply spat on the ground in front of me as I passed.

And then I saw her sitting there at the end of the dock, looking out over the water. Her back was to me as I walked slowly towards her whispering her name under my breath. The people of Harborville must have wondered why their clocks stopped working just then and the men with their boats would not fully recognize why the tide was taking more than its usual time to come back in today. It was my doing. I willed time to stop as I sat down beside the sad girl and did not say a word.

I pulled the four photos from my pocket and set them down on the grey planks between us. I smoothed them out as best I could. "I found these," I said.

She looked only briefly at them and then turned back

to her study of the misty horizon. "I don't know who that little girl is," she said.

"I always hated my school pictures," I said. "My parents always had to buy the complete set. Put them in expensive frames and gave them away to my grandparents, who set them on top of their television. They didn't even seem to care that I had that terrified look on my face. The damn camera caught it every time. It's like my parents couldn't see it. But I could. I hated having my picture taken."

"We didn't take a lot of pictures in my family," Christine said.

"I'm sorry about what happened," I said.

"Well, that's a lot to feel sorry for. But you didn't do it so you have nothing to be sorry for."

"I want to help."

Christine picked up the photos and held them between her fingers, then ripped them down the middle and tossed the fragments out over the water. The scraps fluttered down, landed on the still, dark surface of the harbor and floated delicately on the surface. "The past doesn't exist," she said.

"I agree."

"Neither does the future."

"I agree again. Only the present."

"And there's not much to say about that, is there?"

I looked up and away, felt that stinging in my eyes again, vowed not to show what I was really feeling about the hopelessness of it all.

"The landlord sold the trailer. He had been threatening me, telling me I had to move out but I didn't think he would do it. And then, yesterday, when I walked home, it was gone."

I was thinking about the weather last night. The rain, the wind. "Why didn't you come back to the school?"

"It was my problem, not yours."

"Where did you stay?"

"That's the funny part. I went downtown. I had no plan. Nothing. I was walking down the street. I felt so beaten that I couldn't even bring myself to try to bum money. When I feel strong I can do it. But this was different. I didn't have the strength in me to even beg money from strangers."

She still had not looked at me. Her eyes were fixed, looking up and away over the water. I wondered what she saw out there. "I saw a light was on in the bookshop."

"Mel's?"

"He was there. The door was locked but I tapped on it. He was really loaded. He opened the door. 'Did you read the book?' he asked. `I started it,' I told him. He scared me a little. His breath was, like, overpowering. And he was not all that steady on his feet. I've been around drunken men before. It's not pretty. But he seemed different. I told him I had nowhere to go."

"What did he do?"

"'Stay here,' he said. 'Just don't steal any more books.' I told him about the trailer, how they just towed my home away. He didn't say anything after that. He made me some tea and gave me an apple to eat. Then he left. 'Lock up,' he said and stumbled out into the rain.

"I found the cot in the back room and some blankets. I guess he'd stayed in the store before. I turned off all the store lights and left on a little reading light above the cot. I decided not to think about what would come next but my mind was racing. All I knew was that I had to get away from here. But I kept thinking about you."

"Let me help."

"If you try to help, I'll just drag you down with me."

"No, you won't."

She let out a sigh and turned to look at me. There was an air of total defeat about her. No anger, just defeat. "This morning, when Mel showed up, I think he was surprised to see me. He didn't know what to do. He tried to be polite but he was worried. He was flustered. 'You can't stay on here,' he said. 'A teenage girl living in my store. That's big trouble. Big.' He let me stay until the rain stopped and then I thanked him and left. He was right about me staying there. And about trouble. I'm nothing but bad news."

"That's ridiculous," I said.

"No, it's not. Carson, you're the best thing that ever happened to me. And I'm not going to let me destroy you."

Chapter Twenty

Christine came with me reluctantly to Farnsworth. We went straight to Cromwell's office and I knocked.

"Come in."

We walked in and he looked from me to Christine and then back at me. "She has nowhere to live," I blurted out.

Cromwell was unprepared for this. He seemed unsettled and nervous. It was not like him at all. "Why here? Why now?"

Christine started to tell the story, the long version, but she was having a hard time of it, stumbling over words, stopping to catch her breath. I didn't think she needed to be put through that right now.

"Dr. C.," I interrupted. "She doesn't have any other place to go. Isn't that enough?"

He folded his hands and threaded his fingers together, then leaned on his elbows and touched his thumbs to his forehead. Thinking. I was shocked that he was putting us through this. It wasn't like him at all—the headmaster who was always sure of himself, strong, but also compassionate towards any of us, no matter what the crisis.

"Carson, this is a rather bad time. I think you know about some of it—financial problems and more. We're under a lot of scrutiny right now. And our certification is under review. The timing is terrible, but we're going to have evaluators coming next week. We're not at all prepared for that right now."

"I can take a hint," Christine said and she stood up to go. I reached for her hand but she was already walking to the office door.

"Wait," Cromwell said. "Please." He took a deep breath, changed his tone entirely. "Christine, come back."

She turned to face us, but her hand was still on the doorknob.

"In my line of work, I find that I'm always juggling a complex array of problems." He held his hands out in front of him now and pretended he was literally juggling things. "I realize that I just dropped one the balls I was juggling. The human factor. I apologize."

Christine looked at him but didn't say anything. Then she turned and opened the door and walked out of the room.

I chased after her as she hurried down the stairs. "Wait!" I yelled.

But she didn't stop. Some of the other students were watching now. Doc's little apology had fallen short of the mark. He hadn't handled the situation at all well. Someone was laughing now. One of the girls said, "Carson, aren't you going to introduce us?"

I had to throw myself in front of her and up against the door, blocking her exit. I just stood there breathing hard. I was afraid. Afraid she was going to walk out of there and I'd never see her again.

"Move," she demanded.

"No."

Dr. Cromwell was walking down the stairs now. By now we had a sizeable audience. Christine was standing with her back to everyone but I could see their faces. They were smiling. They didn't get it at all. I wanted to scream at them.

"Everyone," Cromwell announced, "we have a new student here at the Academy. I hope you'll all be generous enough to make Christine feel at home."

Some of the kids mumbled a cursory greeting. Dr. Cromwell casually turned around and went back upstairs. His instincts were good on that. His juggling was back in synch.

Christine lowered her head.

"You hungry?" I asked her.

She nodded. As I eased away from the door, I had a fear that she would bolt. She'd run. So I took her hand and squeezed hard. She'd have to drag me with her if she ran.

Instead, I led her to the one place in the building where I knew she'd feel comfortable.

Mrs. Chin never said hello when anyone walked into the kitchen. Instead, she offered food and gave orders. "Sit," she said. "Eat. Just made some noodle soup. It tastes okay. Not great. Just okay."

She dropped two bowls in front of us and a pair of soupspoons. Mrs. Chin never did anything slowly or carefully. Everything was done with rattling and dropping and the hasty flourish that was her style.

"What kind of soup, is it?"

"Dog soup," she said. "Like back home. Only here, they

don't let me put dog in the soup. So it's dog soup with no dog. But it's not bad."

• • •

Christine was given a room to herself at the far end of the hall from my room. I knew it wasn't going to be easy for her and I was still afraid that she was going to run off. It was nearly nine o'clock that night. I was sitting with her in her room.

"I don't know if I can do this," she said.

"You can."

"Carson, I don't think you understand. I walk around Harborville sometimes and I look at other people. Other families. Mother, father, kids. I can see what they have and I can see that they have lives that make sense. Mine doesn't. Those parents watch their kids grow up and have lives of their own. It's all so perfectly normal. And easy. But my parents . . . I'm not sure they were ever even there for me. And I can't see myself—I can't envision myself—doing anything five years from now. It's too difficult just to make it to tomorrow. This whole school thing here, this isn't going to work. I'll never fit in with those others. Look at me."

I did look at her and I thought she was beautiful. "Don't worry about them. They all have problems. We all have problems. We call this Flunk Out Academy for good reason."

And that's when the cops arrived. Two cars. No sirens but lights flashing. Christine and I went to the window and looked down. This didn't make any sense. I held tightly onto Christine's hand. Suddenly it occurred to me that maybe there was more to her story than I had been willing to accept.

"Oh, my God," she said. "I gotta leave."

"What?" I asked.

Downstairs, the police were already inside the front door. I heard Cromwell leave his office and hurry down the stairs. He confronted the police, demanding an explanation for what was going on.

That familiar look of fear in Christine's eyes. Could they really be after her? And for what? I was afraid to say anything.

I could hear Cromwell arguing with the police as they walked up the stairs. Doors to rooms were opening and closing. Cromwell kept protesting but one of the cops kept repeating, "Just read the damn warrant and shut up."

And then the door opened. I'd seen him in his patrol car before. Mid-thirties, slicked-back black hair, a chin like Clint Eastwood and that self-satisfied smug look on his face. He looked straight at us, let out a funny little snort of breath, a trace of a sick grin.

And then he was gone, moving down the hall to the next room with Cromwell badgering him.

• • •

The cop found Ryan in his room playing a video game and listening to loud music. Against every protest Cromwell could come up with, two policemen ushered Code-X down the stairs and out to the cruiser. Police from the second car were carrying out boxes of something as well. Cromwell was still standing on the front steps shouting at the police when they drove Ryan away.

Cromwell quickly got on the phone to a lawyer and soon drove off. Early in the morning he returned with Ryan in tow. I was asleep on the floor in Christine's room, still afraid to leave her alone. I think she slept deeply and she didn't wake until the sun was up when she woke abruptly. "Where am I?" she gasped.

"It's okay," I said. "It's okay."

She stared at me as she readjusted to consciousness, puzzled at first.

And then she smiled. "You slept there on the floor?"

"Yeah."

"Why?"

"Because I didn't want to leave you."

• • •

The police found the stash of marijuana in the school basement, not particularly well hidden in some old boxes that contained student records from previous years. Code-X had gone for a jump-start to his drug career only the previous week when his father, six months overdue on his son's school fees, finally decided to pay for his son's education. Somehow the wily Code had convinced his folks to make out a cheque in his name which he was supposed to dutifully sign over to the school.

It apparently never occurred to a man like Ryan's father, who ran a corporation worth millions of dollars, that his son might simply cash the cheque and stash the cash. Or in this case, cash the cheque and start his own not-so-legal business enterprise.

Ryan had scored a sizeable amount of hydroponic weed and proceeded to sell off portions of his drug supply to kids in Harborville. He had been in business for less than a week and might have lasted for another week or two (he was not particularly selective about who he sold to, nor was he covert about this illegitimate enterprise), had he not decided to buy a ridiculously large quantity of oregano from the local supermarket and dilute his product. But greed does that to a young entrepreneur and Code-X was one destined to learn everything in life the hard way. One of his dissatisfied customers must have turned him in.

So a few bags of marijuana and some over-the-counter Italian herbs that should have been sprinkled on someone's spaghetti were the straws that broke the camel's back.

It was no coincidence that the fire marshal showed up the next morning and proceeded to come up with a list as long as a man's arm of the things wrong with the school. According to his report, the place was a firetrap and we all should have gone up in smoke a long time ago. This would have been less complicated and only somewhat more tragic than what was about to happen.

• • •

A hastily organized assembly the next morning produced a bleary-eyed Dr. Cromwell and a rather lame attempt to put a positive philosophical spin on the gloomy current state of affairs.

Christine was asleep in her room and I didn't think she needed to be around for it, but I joined the others in the library as the darkest of storm clouds seemed to hover over us within the room.

"What we've known here at Farnsworth," Doc began, "is a way to show love and respect to each other." Sleepy eyes blinked at the notion. It seemed pretty far off the mark, but maybe Cromwell was himself so out of touch with reality that he believed us all to be kind and generous boys and girls instead of selfish, spoiled, hurtful brats.

"We have before us a significant legal and financial challenge and we must close the school until it is sorted out. I'll need you to arrange transportation back to your homes for this afternoon. If you can't work this out then let me know and I will arrange something but, as you can imagine, right now I have my hands full. We'll be in touch when things have been sorted out here so that you can return. It is with much regret that these things must interrupt your studies."

A look of shock was on many of the faces. A couple of girls were crying. Giselle raised her hand but didn't wait to be called on. "When can we come back?" she asked.

Cromwell put his hands out in front of him, palms up.

For many of us, "going home" did not have the cosy ring to it that it might for a well-adjusted kid heading home from summer camp. There were various and serious reasons why home had not been a healthy environment for us. That was why we were here.

Ryan, bailed out of jail and sitting there in the midst of us, must have felt the wrath of his classmates who blamed him for the current sordid turn of affairs. He blurted out, "I can't go home. Not now."

"You have no choice," Cromwell answered in a level voice.

"This sucks," Mary said. "We didn't do anything to deserve this." Meaning that Ryan did but the rest of us were guiltless. The punishment did not fit the crime. Our communal crimes were mostly behind us. Farnsworth, our beloved Flunk Out Academy, was the institution that had saved our sorry asses from the terror of living in the outside world. Here we had safe haven and asylum. And now it was about to be ripped away from us.

It's hard to explain why someone didn't come out and shout something obscene at Ryan. Instead, an awful silence fell over the assembled. Finally, Ryan got up and began to walk out of the room. "It's not fair," he said out loud. "It wasn't my fault." He sounded like a little boy who had just broken a window or dropped his glass of milk. But Ryan was worrying about Ryan. He didn't give a rat's ass about the rest of us.

I sneaked a sideways glance at Fin and saw genuine fear in his face. He was not alone. Others had stone faces of disbelief and shock. Some were angry. "Fin," I whispered. "It'll be okay." I don't know why I said it because I didn't believe the words at all. I guess I had tried in my own way to be like a brother to Fin. Not that I'd been more together than he was. We had been a couple of lonely, unhappy campers from the get-go. But now we each would have to deal with this disaster in our own ways.

"No, it won't," Fin said in an low but angry voice. "TEOTWAWKI." And he headed upstairs to pack.

• • •

Christine had not attended the gathering but was awake when I returned to visit her. She was brushing her hair in front of the mirror.

"They're closing the school," I said with an air of defeat. "Everyone is going to have to leave."

"And you're going to go home, right?"

I studied her in the morning light. Despite the bad news morning, there was something about her that was radiant. Beautiful. She still carried all the weight of the sadness of her life, but right here, right at this one moment with both of us together in the quiet room, everything seemed fine. This was in no way logical. In a metaphorical sense, the walls of the old mansion were collapsing as we spoke. The school was crumbling. The one steady and reliable thing in my world was falling into a chasm in the earth, never to emerge again.

"No, I can't go home," I told her.

"Neither can I," she said.

• • •

Curiously enough, Ryan's father showed up first. I guess his son had finally gotten his attention. Mr. Luger, a thin man with a determined air about him, breezed into the school, had a small audience with Dr. Cromwell and then collected his son and his bags. Ryan didn't say goodbye to anyone and no one said good bye to him. Ryan was leaving this place and about to go out into the world where he would no doubt inflict damage on himself and on whoever he came in contact with. There was a terrible inevitability to it. His father checked his watch as he opened the door to his BMW and slid in beside the wheel. I wondered if he had paid Dr. Cromwell back the money the headmaster had put up for Ryan's bail. Or were both the Lugers members of that breed of men who wreak havoc, take advantage of the goodwill of others, and then just move on down the road, never to look back?

• • •

Dr. Cromwell tried his best to get each student into his office for a brief good-bye. I had been thinking I might do well to simply avoid him, but he came while Fin was out of the room and he sat on the edge of the bed, trying his best not to look like the world's most defeated man.

"Carson," he said. "What's your plan?"

"I guess I'll go home," I lied.

"Your friend, Christine?"

"Oh, she phoned up an aunt of hers and it turns out she can stay there." I was amazed that I could lie like this and he couldn't detect it. I'd always had this feeling that Cromwell understood everything about each of us, that he knew when we were telling the truth and when we were lying. But now I could see he was much more mortal than I had believed. "What about you?" I asked as if I were speaking to a friend and not the headmaster.

He ruffled a hand through his hair and then stroked his chin. "Sort out the mess here, I suppose. Try to regroup. It wasn't just Ryan, you know. I knew that one day, something would happen to draw attention to us. There were people in this town just waiting for an excuse to close us down. I'm going to have to relocate. But that will take a little time."

"I'll miss this place," I said. "I really will." There was no lying in that.

"We all will." He held a hand up now and swallowed, shifted in his seat so he could look out the window at a blue jay that was sitting on the branch there. "Carson, I'm overstepping my bounds but I have to tell you what I think about Christine."

"You already told me."

"Well, it's just that you need to know why a person does that to herself."

"I understand that she wanted to hurt herself. I think I can understand that. You feel so bad that you want to damage . . . something. In her case it was herself. I think she's okay now, though."

"I'm glad you are her friend. I really am. But you have to be careful she doesn't drag you down, too."

"What do you mean?"

"The self-inflicted damage she did—it comes from feeling shame and worthlessness. And fear."

"She's had a rough life."

"I know that. I understand that things went wrong with her parents. She may blame herself no matter how illogical that may seem. Instead of her getting angry at her parents and rebelling in any number of ways, she took it out on herself. And sometimes, once people start injuring themselves, they discover that it gets them attention and part of them likes that."

"You're saying she drove things into her arms to get people to pay attention to her?"

"It could be. She needs some serious professional help. I'm sure of it."

"But I don't think that is going to happen. I don't think she would trust anyone to help her."

"Anyone but you, right?"

"I want to help her."

"But there is a risk. For you."

"How?"

"You could buy into her way of looking at the world."

Doc was scaring me with the intense way he was looking at me now. I wanted him to back off. "Oh, and I suppose I should instead stay clear of her and live in a different world, a rosy little place where everything turns out okay in the end. Happily ever after."

"No, I'm not sure that world exists."

"Then what are you saying?"

"I'm saying you need to be careful. If you are going to remain her friend, you need to keep a strong hold on who you are and what you believe."

Cromwell said this as if he believed I had a strong grasp of my own identity and direction in life. "Okay." I said. "I can do that."

"Good," he said. "I think you are strong and fine." He held out his hand for me to shake.

Strong and fine. Odd words. "Good luck, Carson."

"Thanks."

As I got up to go, I thought he might give me a hug but he didn't. As I was leaving, he turned away from me and looked out the window again. The blue jay had flown off and Doctor Cromwell closed his eyes.

Chapter Twenty-one

When I said goodbye to Fin, he was packing up his computer. I promised I'd drop into his chat room or send him an e-mail. He knew I hated computers and probably would never do this, but he said nothing, just kept wrapping up wires into neat little bundles and putting rubber bands around them. I wanted to tell Fin what I had planned, but decided it was better to tell no one.

I guess Dr. C. was plain overwhelmed with the details of closing down the school. He had told each of us to call our parents and tell them to come pick us up. For some strange reason he trusted us to do this simple task. But I knew what I had to do. I did not call them as I was supposed to do. As of that moment, they did not know about the closure of the school yet and they would not be coming. They would be frantic about my disappearance and I felt a twinge of guilt. But I knew what I had to do. And, as we liked to say around FOA, they'd get over it.

I packed my large backpack and a small suitcase. The rest of my stuff, I just left in my room. Christine left first. "Meet me at Mel's bookstore," I said. I figured it would be less likely that we'd get noticed if we left separately. Downstairs, parents were showing up. Some of the kids looked sullen; others started arguing with the adults right away. Dr. Cromwell was noticeably absent.

Fin gave me a funny look as I put my backpack on. "I'll be back for the rest," I said. Then I walked quickly downstairs and headed out the back way, through the kitchen. Mrs. Chin was at the sink. I didn't say anything and, for a second, I thought she wouldn't notice me. But I was wrong.

"Carson," she snapped.

I stopped dead in my tracks.

"Just wanted to avoid the crowd out front," I said guiltily.

"How much do you need?"

"What do you mean?"

"Money. You have enough money?"

"What are you talking about? I'm going home."

"Here," she said pulling out a wad of bills from her apron pocket. "Take this."

She looked at me straight in the eye. I'm not sure she had ever done this before. I reached out and took the money. Before she let go, she pulled me towards her and gave me a bear hug that stopped me from breathing. Then she let go. "You are good," she said and turned away.

"Thanks," I said. I pocketed the money and slipped out the back door. In a minute, I had edged around back of the garage and then slipped through a hedge. I walked through a couple of back yards and then headed downtown.

• • •

Now, all my life I'd read about and heard about the mythology of "running away." Little kids got mad at their parents and started walking down the street with some kind of favorite stuffed animal under their arm. Older kids got in trouble and fled to avoid facing up to their petty crimes.

But this was different.

With Farnsworth DOA, and with nothing but a bleak future at home and a steady parade to shrinks and pharmacies to cope with depression, I felt I had no other choice than to "start a new life." Another tidy little myth read about in books and seen on TV.

In order to start that new life, someone had to go somewhere and I had no idea where we were going. So far, the first stop was Mel's Used Books. Maybe Mel would have some sodden advice. Right.

And then a stab of fear shot through me. What if Christine was not at Mel's? What if she decided she was better off without me?

I envisioned myself all too clearly standing there in the store. Mel with a sad concerned look on his face as I cracked and crumbled into dust before him. I was pretty far out on a limb and I hadn't fully realized it. Running from? Running to? Or just running?

● ● ●

That silly little bell rang when I opened the door to the store. Mel was sitting in a chair, reading. Christine was nowhere to be seen.

Mel looked up, didn't seem at all surprised. He tipped the book forward. "*The Meditations of Marcus Aurelius*. I've been putting it off for years."

"Is she here?"

"Who?"

"Christine."

"Haven't seen her since the other night. She okay?"

"I don't know." It was like the blood was draining out of my head down into my body. Christine was not here as promised. She was gone. Soon, all of me would seep into the floorboards and sink into the earth. What had I been thinking?

Mel didn't know what to say. He turned back to his book and read. "'Though thou shouldst be going to live three thousand years, or as many as ten thousand years, still remember that no man loses any other life than this which he now lives, nor lives any other than this which he now loses. The longest and the shortest are thus brought to the same. For the present is the same to all.' Amen, brother."

I wasn't really listening to what he read. Things had an odd, unreal quality and I began to see that this new transformed me had been a temporary thing. A kind of crazy chemical imbalance brought on by . . . by Christine and the time I'd spent with her? I had been betrayed. And now I moved it all back onto the inventory of the things I hated in this world.

"Carson," Mel said. "You in trouble?"

"Yeah."

"You weren't the one with the dope at the school?"

"No," I answered.

"They're closing the place, aren't they?"

"Yes."

"The bastards. You know, some people in this town have wanted that place out of existence ever since Cromwell opened it. It wasn't because the place was falling down. And it wasn't because it was the home of a bunch of snot-nosed rich kids, either. Nope. It wasn't that at all."

I didn't really care what it was. I looked at the shelves of books and wondered why anyone would have gone to so much effort to write them, to spend their days writing anything as pointless and useless as a book.

"It was Cromwell himself. They wanted to see him fail."

I looked up at Mel. He put a liquor store receipt in between the pages of Marcus Aurelius and looked past me, out to the people walking by on Main Street. "Poor crazy Richard."

"Crazy?"

"Well, we all thought so. He grew up here, ya know, before he went away. He was a couple of years younger than me, but I remember him at school. The kids in this town tore him apart. He was funny-looking. He was different. He had these crazy ideas and he wasn't afraid to tell anyone. And he was smarter than the lot of us. And so we crucified him for it.

"He went away to university out west and then to freaking England. When we heard about him getting a doctorate, we all laughed like hyenas. Even me."

"Why?"

"Because that's the kinda people we were. It seemed like a joke. How could screwed-up little Richard Cromwell get a bleeding PhD from one of the most famous universities in the world? And I was ignorant enough to laugh with the worst of the snivelling twits.

"But then he came back here . . . and opened up that school. Well, that was different. I myself shook my head and thought it ludicrous but the others . . . some couldn't abide by it. They thought he was trying to prove he was better than us. And they wanted him to hang."

"And now they have their wish," I said. It took my mind off Christine, however briefly. I wondered what would become of Dr. C. I thought of the hard times that all the kids had given him. I remembered what he had revealed about his own problems as a kid. And I realized that he had opened up his precious academy for the lost because he himself had been—or still was—one of us.

• • •

I was looking out the window when I saw her. She had three plastic shopping bags and she was crossing the street. She was coming here.

The bell over the door rang and she spilled into the room in a shower of sunlight. At first I couldn't believe it was really her.

She saw the look on my face. "Carson, you okay?"

I couldn't move.

She held her bags up. "Everything is wet and dirty. I don't know why but I wanted some of my things. When I first saw all my stuff heaved in the trash there by the dumpster, I didn't care. I didn't care what they did to me. But now . . . it's different. I do care about some things. I walked back there and, with my old neighbors watching, I rooted through my stuff. I was down on my hands and knees and some of the little kids rode up on their bikes and asked me what I was doing. So I told them.

"But their parents. They just stood back and watched. I took my time. Found what I was looking for and then came back here." She spilled the contents of her bags onto the floor. Dirty, wet clothes. Familiar flannel shirts and jeans and a pair of dirty runners that looked like they belonged to someone else. They were way too small for her.

Christine picked them up and showed them to me. "I'd almost forgotten," she said. "A few years back, when things were bad. Really bad. I would put these on and run. No one knew where I went but I ran through fields and along the edge of the inlet, as far out of town as I could get. I ran until it stopped hurting."

Some Harborvillains were walking by the window just then and they stopped to look at us. It probably wasn't much more than idle curiosity the way they stood there and squinted their eyes, peering in at us. But Mel didn't like it at all. He tapped on the glass of the window and held up his fist like a madman.

As they started to walk away, he muttered. "The bastards. The dirty, rotten bastards."

Chapter Twenty-two

Christine lifted her old running shoes and stared at them. "When I felt really bad, I would just run. As far as I could. I don't know why I stopped running. It made me feel that good. And it made me feel free. I used to run far up the inlet until I was totally exhausted. There's an old cabin up there. I stayed overnight there a couple of times. And you know what? No one even missed me."

"You stayed alone?" I asked.

"It was scary but I trained myself to deal with that. It was used by hunters in the fall, but I never saw anyone else there at any other time of the year."

"We need supplies," I said, pulling the money Mrs. Chin had given me out of my pocket. I was shocked to discover she had given me fifty dollars.

Mel was rooting around in his back room now. I heard him mutter, "Son of a bitch." He emerged with an old beat-up rucksack on an aluminum carrying frame. He handed it to Christine. "Do you believe it? I used to climb mountains."

"Really?" I asked. "Where?"

Mel shrugged. "Everywhere. Rockies. Alps. Went to Nepal

once. My dream was to climb one of those peaks close to Everest. I didn't need to go up the big one. I just wanted to get into the rafters of the roof of the world. But I had to give up climbing."

"Why?" Christine asked.

"I was afraid of heights. Had been ever since I was a kid. That's why I started climbing. Confront what you fear most. That was my motto. But then one day, halfway up a mountain in Alaska, it caught up with me. Scared the bejeezus out of me. I became paralysed with fear. My companions had to literally carry me down out of there. Never went up a mountain since. Enjoy the pack. It's been around the world twice."

Before we left Mel's store, he picked a paperback from the shelves. "*Walden*," he said. "Henry David Thoreau. You might need it." He dropped it into his old rucksack. "Be good to each other," he said as the little bell rang and we were out the door.

• • •

In the IGA store, Christine took charge. I was pretty fuzzy on what we should be buying to keep us alive in the woods. Christine seemed to have it all figured out. It was like a super-lesson in frugal survival shopping. "Trust me. I've had to figure out how to live on next to nothing. I hope you like rice."

"Not really," I said.

"You'll learn to love it."

She hefted a large bag of dried rice into the cart. And dried beans. "Think of it as Mexican cuisine," she said, having suddenly developed a sense of both authority and humor.

182

There were other equally unpalatable looking packs of dried goods—more beans, and peas, and something called lentils, some almost friendly-looking pastas and noodles. And small clear bags of spices dipped from bulk bins. "Tricks of the trade," she said.

There were some cans and dried goods and a sorry assortment of other unhappy looking foodstuffs and I decided to keep my mouth shut lest I suggest we stock up on junk food. It was as if she had had this whole thing planned out—or maybe it was just the years of experience of going it on her own.

And when the cashier tallied up the total and it came to $49.87, I nearly freaked. She had been keeping a running total in her head the whole time. I handed over the fifty bucks and accepted my dime and three pennies in change. "We can't buy anything where we're going anyway," Christine said.

Outside the store, we loaded up both our packs as best we could and each carried what was left in doubled-up grocery store plastic bags. We looked like a couple of hobos. "Let's head down to the harbor and walk along the shore. It will take longer than the road but we'd be better off the beaten track."

• • •

When we walked past the place where Christine and I had slid down the mud on that sun-drenched day we both smiled but said nothing. I tapped her on the shoulder to stop though, and I kissed her on the mouth. She liked it. And so did I. I was beginning to think that this is what we could do in our spare time. Up above, seagulls wheeled in the light breeze. The sky was blue, and higher up I could see the white vapor trails of jets. I felt like we were leaving behind the civilized world, the world as we knew it. Right then, for only the splittest of split seconds, I felt totally alive. And totally free.

We walked for four hours. My feet and back were sore. I had deep ridges in my hands from carrying those damn plastic bags that dug into my skin. I had to stop and rest four times. Christine didn't sit down when I stopped. Instead, she remained standing. Each time I grew tired, I felt fear creeping up my spine. "Do we know what we are doing?" I asked tentatively.

"I think so," she said. "This was my backup plan. I didn't even know I had one until I visited your school. I didn't really think they'd let me stay there."

"I bet I could have talked Doc into it."

"It doesn't matter now. There's no school to go back to."

"So long, Flunk Out Academy," I said, getting shakily back onto my feet. "Which way?" I asked. It was a joke. We'd been following the inlet off the big harbor. There was only one way to go.

"Just follow the yellow brick road," she said.

"You used to run this far?"

"We've got another hour to go at this pace."

"What do you mean *at this pace*?"

"Sorry. I used to run out here. I never walked."

Running from or running to? I wanted to ask but didn't want to say it out loud. It applied all too well to my current inner quandary. Running from or running to? Maybe it amounted to the same thing.

We grew quieter as we walked. Not that we'd ever been very talkative, either one of us. It was a beautiful afternoon and it felt like the world's greatest adventure. I thought about Mel. About mountain climbing. I couldn't picture him as being young and athletic. It just didn't fit. Christine walked beside me sometimes and sometimes in front of me. Leading me. I couldn't believe I had come to trust her so deeply. And that she had trusted me.

And then the doubts would set in. Where were we going anyway? What if there was no cabin there? She said it had been a few years since she'd been there. What are we going to do about water? About bathrooms? About . . . well, everything? Once the train of doubt leaves the station, it's amazing how much speed it can pick up. The little whining voice inside my head grew louder and louder and I couldn't shake it when it started to ask, "What will your mom and dad think? Imagine how they are going to feel." Part of me wished that I had phoned them from town just to say I was okay and to let them know I hadn't fallen off the edge of the world. But I was afraid they'd talk me out of it. I was afraid I'd crack.

The inlet had narrowed and, above the waterline, there was a marsh with green low-lying grasses. Up ahead were two ducks with five babies trailing behind them in the water. "In the fall, the hunters come here and shoot them."

"How could they?" I asked. "They look so peaceful and beautiful."

Christine shrugged. I tried not to think about baby ducks growing up for one happy healthy summer and then, suddenly, men with guns coming out from town and killing them.

And then we were there.

"Oh, my God," I said out loud. I guess I had imagined something like a well-kept hunter's lodge. I don't know why but I did. This was a tar paper shack. It looked like it was on a tilt, as if it were sinking into the ground it stood on. It was smaller than I had anticipated—a true one-room shack. A metal stovepipe protruded through the roof. Shingles were missing. The glass in the front windows was cracked. And someone or something had wrenched the door so that it was hanging by one hinge. My heart sank.

"What do you think?" Christine asked.

I swallowed hard. "I love it," I said. And she dropped her pack and hugged me so hard that I couldn't breathe.

Chapter Twenty-three

Christine busted off the small padlock by kicking it. She opened the door and we inspected the inside of our new home. It was primitive but not impossible. Funny that it made me think of my father when he used to talk about "moving back to the land." You couldn't get much closer to "the land" than this.

I pretended I wasn't scared but a part of me was. My parents would not know what happened to me. They probably didn't deserve that but I felt that I had no other choice. If I walked away from Christine, I knew I'd never see her again. And I didn't want to lose her. Ever.

We drank water from the well behind the cabin but not before Christine had convinced me to boil it in a pot on the cook stove. There were pots and pans here and some blankets to sleep under on the musty old bunk bed. I used the axe to chop up wood for a fire in the cook stove.

After the sun went down, we lit a few candles that we had bought and I kept the fire going. We both grew strangely quiet. We fell asleep with our clothes on sitting on the lower bunk bed and I was awakened by Christine shouting something in her sleep. I opened my eyes to total darkness and, at first, I didn't know where I was or what was going on. If she was dreaming, it was a very bad dream.

"Christine," I whispered. "Wake up. Wake up please."

But she didn't wake up. She started to shout louder, "No! No!"

That was when I became terrified. I didn't know what to do, how to help her. I shook her gently and whispered her name over and over.

And then she stopped screaming and she began to sob. I couldn't see her face at all in the dark. "Are you okay?" I asked.

"I'm sorry," she said. "I should have warned you."

"About what?"

"About me. About the dreams. I can't even remember them when I wake up. It's like something terrible is happening but I don't know what it is. I just know I'm terrified. And in the dreams, I have no place to go that is safe. I want to hide but I can't. I don't even know who I'm trying to hide from. It's not like there is someone in the dream who is trying to hurt me. It's not that."

"What is it then?"

"It's that I'm afraid of being alone. When I was young, I'd come home and no one would be there. My father would be gone and my mother would not show up sometimes for hours and I'd put myself to bed and tell myself it was going to be okay. But I was so scared."

"You're not alone now. I'll stay with you."

"I want to stay with you forever," she said, snuggling in my arms.

Part of me knew that we were living in a little fantasy. The world would catch up with us. That world that I once so much detested. It—some form of it—would find us and tell us we could not do what we were doing. And that seemed so unfair.

"I'll be back," I said, not wanting her to know what I was thinking. I needed a breath of fresh air to fix my brain. And I needed to pee.

I walked outside and took a few tentative steps away from the house. I peed in the clearing in front of the cabin. And it all seemed unreal.

And then I looked up. "My God," I said out loud. "Christine, come out here."

In a second she was out the door, with the blanket still wrapped around her. And I said, "Look up."

There were a million stars, a million stunning crystals of light in the night sky. "It's beautiful," she said.

"It is beautiful," I said and the sound of the word seemed very odd. I realized it was not a word I used. Ever. But now I said it again. "Beautiful."

I held her in my arms as she wrapped the blanket around both of us. I wanted time to stand still. I wanted the rest of the world to forget about us, and leave us alone. For a few brief minutes, with my cheek against hers, with the night sky exploding with stars above our heads, I felt the thrill of being alive.

"It's like I've been living in a trance up until this minute," I said. "It's like I've only been half alive."

She didn't say anything at first. Then she spoke. "Let's go back in. I've got to tell you something but I can't do it when you are looking at me. Maybe I can do it in the dark.

"Okay."

We clumsily stumbled back into the cabin, found the bunk in the dark, and I wrapped the blanket around us as we sat close together.

"I was thinking tonight, before I fell asleep, that I might spare you a lot of grief if I just left. Disappeared."

After all we had gone through today to get here, this didn't seem to make any sense. Hearing her say this also shook me in a way that made the room spin. One minute, I'm happier than I've ever been my whole life, and now it seemed like this girl and this night could all vanish like a dream. "Why?" I asked.

"My life has never been easy,"

"Maybe there's no such thing as an easy life. For anyone."

"I know you've had things tough, too. But you also had parents who were there. I could tell from meeting them once that they loved you."

I laughed. "And that's part of why I felt like such a shit every time I let them down."

"But they still loved you."

"I know they did."

"I didn't have that," she said. "My parents were in it for themselves. I can't remember what it was like when I was a baby. Someone must have raised me. Maybe my mother loved me then. But early on, I knew I was pretty much on my own. And that did something to me."

"You survived, though."

"Just barely. Feel my arm."

I had tried to forget about that. Here, holding her in the dark, that part had been easy. But now she slid my hand down her right arm and I could feel the scars. I remember what Dr. Cromwell had told me about this. I could hear his words ring in my head.

"You can't scare me off, you know," I said.

"Maybe not. But I need to tell you this."

I held onto her arm. I brushed my fingers gently over those scars that I could not see in the darkness.

"I didn't have any real friends and my mother seemed to just drop in and out of my life, leaving me on my own more and more often and I guess, in a way, I got used to it. But something in me *always* felt unloved, rejected. And then I began to believe that she and my father weren't around because there was something wrong with me. It was my fault.

"And I came to the conclusion that everyone else was normal—all those other kids in school with their mommies and daddies—but me, I was just not as good as them. So I started hating me. And I started doing things. I cut myself with a kitchen knife. I pretended at first it was an accident. But then I took a paper clip and pushed it into my arm. It hurt but it also felt good. I liked it."

I held her more tightly and said nothing. I closed my eyes and pretended I could still see those stars up over the cabin. "You don't have to tell me all this if you don't want to."

"You need to hear it. If you still feel that you want me to stay, you need to hear it. If you change your mind after that it will be okay, it really will."

"Okay."

"Sometimes, alone at night, having worn myself out from hating myself for an entire day, I'd get to a point where I stopped feeling bad and I felt nothing at all. I felt empty. That was even worse. So then I'd find some way to hurt myself again, to feel the physical pain because feeling that pain was somehow better than feeling nothing. That's how messed up I was."

"I'm so sorry," I said. "Do you still . . . um . . . ?" but I couldn't make myself ask the question.

"No," she said. "I haven't for a long time. I want to sometimes but I don't. I went to get help but I'm not sure any of it did any good. Sooner or later, I'd find that I was back on my own again. Social Services got involved for a while but my mother, when she was around, convinced them everything was okay even though she knew what I had been doing to myself. And then she'd be back in the trailer with me for a week or a month. Then she would disappear again and phone from a bar somewhere telling me that she was off on her next adventure with a new boyfriend. It's been like that for a long time." She stopped and the wind in the treetops was all you could hear. She took a deep breath. "And then you came along."

I didn't know what to say.

"Bet you feel like running," Christine said.

Part of me did. A voice inside my head was telling me: all I had to do was leave here and go back home. I knew my parents would be mad at me but they would take me back. I could return to the safe and nearly comfortable role of being the family loser that I had always been. I'd worked long and hard at those skills of pushing away the world I hated and turning my back on the people in it. Maybe that was what I was supposed to continue to do with the rest of my life.

And now this.

"I feel like sleeping," I said. I fixed the blanket around us and kept my arm wrapped around her shoulder. "You're not alone now," I said. "I'm right here and I'm not going anywhere."

But we didn't go to sleep. Christine kissed me on my lips and then on my neck. I slipped my arms down around her and held her even more tightly to me. And soon I could tell by the way she moved against me that she wanted me. We both seemed to totally trust the other. She was the one leading the way.

It was the first time I had ever made love to a girl. I don't know if it was her first time but I guessed it wasn't. Among her "supplies" were condoms and I can't imagine when it was she had added them to our stash. All I know is that it was intense and in our lovemaking I gave myself totally to her. I think it changed something inside me in a deep and powerful way. It was sex, yes, but it was something much more than that.

Chapter Twenty-four

When I awoke in the morning, I was alone. I was still half sitting up and the blanket was wrapped tightly around me. The cabin was cold and I waited for consciousness to seep into my brain. Christine was not in the cabin and I did something I had not done for a long time.

I prayed that she had not left me here alone. But I braced myself for the very real possibility. I recalled instantly all she had told me the night before. The girl had some heavy emotional baggage. And wherever she decided to go in life that baggage would be with her no matter how light she tried to travel or how far she tried to run. "Please, God . . ." I heard myself say out loud. All I really wanted was a miracle.

With the blanket still wrapped around my shoulders, I opened the door and walked out into the morning.

The sun was just rising over the nearby inlet and I walked towards it slowly, fighting back tears. Birds were singing and the ground felt cool and damp on my bare feet. As I followed the path I wanted badly to shout out her name but my throat felt dry and I didn't have the energy to even whisper.

And then I saw her.

Standing on the shoreline of the inlet, with her arms wrapped around herself, silhouetted by the rising sun. She heard me walking towards her and turned.

"I was sound asleep," she said, "and then I felt it touching my face, the very first light of the sun coming in through the window."

"And now this," she said pointing at the sun so bold and golden over the water and the marsh. Seagulls, ravens, and ducks swirled in the sky.

"I've never seen anything like it," I said. All my life, I'd never had the pleasure of standing on a shoreline at sunrise. First the stars and then this. "It's perfect," I said, maybe an odd choice of words.

"It *is* perfect," she echoed. "And it's my birthday."

"You're kidding."

"No. I wasn't going to tell you. Until I saw this and then I knew I had to tell you. I'm seventeen today."

I remembered she'd told me before that soon she'd be seventeen. It was a big turning point in anyone's life but I knew what it implied—at least in Christine's mind. She would be considered to be an adult if she cared to be—her mother, Social Services, schools would no longer have much interest in her welfare. Not that they'd been paying much attention or helping her along. But, like she had said, she'd be free to go wherever she wanted and do whatever she decided to do.

"How'd you do that?" I asked.

"Do what?"

I pointed to the sun rising over the inlet.

"The same way you did the stars," she said.

I felt sure now of some things. I felt optimistic. I was beginning to believe that we were somehow responsible for our own happiness now. Not the rest of the world. Not them. Us. "You know what we are doing out here, don't you?"

"Living in the woods," she said, smiling now, the sun soft and warm on her beautiful face.

"Well, that. But more. We're fixing the world. We're putting everything back to the way it should be. I did the stars. You did this. What's next?" That's the way I felt. It was like a job we'd been guided to do.

"God, I love all this," she said, her arms out wide.

"Me too," I said.

• • •

We ate some dry granola for breakfast and made tea on the cook stove, me coughing from the smoke when I lifted the lid to put in more pieces of pine wood. I'd never eaten granola before in my life. It made me think of my parents who had been trying to make me eat granola and muesli for years. Not once had I taken them up on it. And now I had discovered that it wasn't that bad.

I was coming close to admitting that there was a long and growing list of things I did not hate in the world. And a shorter, but still substantial, list of things that I downright loved.

We sat down on the grass outside after that and Christine brought out the book Mel had given her. *Walden* by Henry David Thoreau. She read out loud to me: "I went to the woods because I wished to live deliberately, to front the essential facts of life and see if I could not learn what it had to teach and not, when it came time to die, discover that I had not lived."

She stopped right there. I felt the skin tighten over the back of my skull. "Good ole Mel," I said.

There were red squirrels now chattering at us from the trees and sparrows flitting about. I could see a hawk flying high over the marsh. "Happy birthday," I said. "I forgot to say happy birthday."

"I've never really had anyone that I wanted to celebrate my birthday with before—not since I was very little anyway. It was one of those things that other kids took for granted. But not me. I used to lie to kids about having a birthday party or getting presents."

"Damn," I said.

"Damn what?"

"I don't have a present for you."

"You didn't know."

"But we'll do something special."

"This is something special," she said.

● ● ●

I guess it will sound plenty screwy what I'm about to say next. But it was all new emotional geography to me and I had a hard time believing that it was familiar to those other normal people who supposedly populated this planet. "So this is happiness?" I said out loud.

Christine laughed. "I guess it is."

Now, once you've come out and said anything that definite, that absolute, that corny, it sets you thinking about how you can keep things just as they are and not change a thing. And as soon as you think about that, you realize you can't do it. Something will have to give.

And it did.

• • •

Christine read some more Thoreau to me out loud. Although the language was a bit odd, it made a lot of sense. But in a way, it also *didn't* make sense. If he were right about how our lives were "frittered away by detail," then why the hell didn't we stick with the "essentials"? Out here in the woods I was beginning to get some idea as to what the essentials were. I talked about this with Christine and we both felt a kind of confusion settle over us. We had barely just learned to live in the moment and just as quickly realized that we couldn't hold onto it.

The past was chasing her and the future was pestering me. Through the day, we found several lucky moments when we slipped back into the here-and-now, but just as quickly and more often, we grew silent and sullen. We had entered a new country, crossed over some border, slipped through immigration but we did not know the language or the laws of the land we were living in.

It rained that night and the roof leaked. I stoked the fire to keep us warm and settled pots into locations to catch the drips but the leaks kept moving from one location to another all night. Christine slept hardly at all the night of her seventeenth birthday and I fell into fitful catnaps only to be awakened by the ding of rainwater dripping into a well-placed pot.

It rained all the next day and I found myself out in it trying to split damp firewood to keep up a fire inside.

On the third day, we had given up on Thoreau and rather wished we had electricity, running water, and central heating. It was a sodden, cold day and the magic of rustic life was not returning. I was having second thoughts about being out here and I couldn't persuade Christine to tell me what she was thinking.

"You need to call your parents and tell them you are okay. You owe that to them," she finally blurted out even though we had not been discussing this issue at all.

I wanted to say that I didn't owe them anything but it wasn't true. My parents had been good to me. I had sometimes wished my parents were mean and terrible people so I could have felt justified in the way I felt towards them but it wasn't like that. And Christine's words tweaked my growing guilt. I had disappeared. They didn't know what had happened to me and they were suffering. It was the least I could do.

We took a path through the woods that led to the road from Harborville to Easton. Christine led me to a gas station and, inside, in the gas station office, the guy working there let me use their phone. He watched us and listened to everything I said to my mom who had answered the phone. She was crying on the other end. But I tried not to let that get to me. I told her what she needed to know. "I'm okay," I said. "I've got a good place to stay and I don't think I can come home. But I'll call you once in a while. I really am fine. I'm sorry." And I hung up.

The guy behind the desk gave me a dirty look. I wondered if he thought I was some kind of criminal.

"Thanks for letting me use the phone," I said.

"Don't mention it," he said but he looked like he had formed a pretty severe opinion of who I was and what I was up to. I felt his look burn a hole right through me.

Christine and I headed away from there in the opposite direction from where the cabin was and then we doubled back through the woods. When we arrived at the cabin, it felt different somehow. Just walking out to the highway, talking to my tearful mom, and then coming back here made me feel like I had somehow physically reconnected us to the rest of the outside world. It was like we had figured out how to make that world go away, but now it was back.

Chapter Twenty-five

We walked out on the clear nights and located the Milky Way, identified a couple of constellations, and pointed out satellites moving like pretend stars in the dark sky. I quoted the line I'd found in Thoreau about "the sky pebbly with stars," and she laughed. Christine somehow knew how to wake me right at sunrise and drag me out to the shoreline where we tempted blindness by staring into the sun as it lifted itself up from the horizon and began to climb its invisible massive ladder up into the sky. With each new day we pushed the outside world back away from us and got to know each other better than I could ever have believed possible.

I'd known of other guys having girlfriends and I'd heard them talk. I knew something remotely about relationships from television and movies and from watching others my age. But this was different. And the words fail me here. We had tender physical moments but those were not the highlights. Instead, we watched out for each other. We understood our common ground. We were each refugee and refuge. Each of us was both a wounded victim and a healer. We soon lost track of the date, and after that we did not know which day of the week it was. We went to bed with the setting sun and we rose with it again the next day.

We had only one book and read from it out loud when a passage caught our fancy—sometimes cutting a silence so profound that it seemed almost tangible, something you could touch. "When we are unhurried and wise, we perceive that only great and worthy things have any permanent and absolute existence . . ."

"Are we unhurried and wise?" she'd ask.

"Almost," I said. "I think we are getting there."

We made fun of Thoreau even as we borrowed his language. He was after all from another century. And his book was one we might have been forced to read in school. Had that been the case, I don't think I would have liked it. But this was different.

There were fishing poles in the cabin and we'd both been thinking about how to feed ourselves better without another trip to town to spend our last few dollars, what was left of my parents' school allowance that I had kept in reserve for an emergency. Our diet had been less than exciting and I had craved for junk food, for pizza, and for a cheeseburger. Instead of sneaking off to a McDonald's for a Big Mac (as I sometimes fantasized), I dug worms from the dark soil near the inlet and held them up wriggling. "These are great and worthy things," I suggested, all the while feeling a tinge of guilt over the fact that we would use them as bait. But they served us well and we thanked both them and the fish we caught for their sacrifice.

Unhurried and wise was the way we fished. We had learned in a few short days to abandon the time measures of the twenty-first century. I could not tell you the names of the fish we caught but they tasted exquisite—this from a kid who had once hated any form of seafood.

And there were clams to be dug with the broken shovel. From the flour Christine had insisted we buy, she made some kind of Indian flatbread that she called chapatti, that I learned to love—freshly fried in a pan or dry and crisp like a cracker. Our days were filled with the necessary activities of our survival. And those days were also filled with wonder.

•   •   •

I was gathering firewood for cooking when they arrived.

My father and mother came hiking our way, both with red backpacks along the trail by the inlet. They saw us before I saw them. My father waved as they walked slowly and purposely towards us.

I went through a time shift just then. I suddenly wondered exactly how long we had been here in the woods. More than a week, possibly ten days. I honestly didn't know although, in my bones, it seemed as if Christine and I had been living here for a lifetime. Our strange and wonderful happiness had lasted that long.

I drove the axe into a large soft log, left it there and then took a few steps forward. My mother reached out first and pulled me into an embrace. My father joined in until I felt nearly smothered by both of them. A profound sense of confusion swept over me. Guilt for having abandoned them. But also love. It was good to see them.

Christine hovered by the door of the cabin, understanding somewhat what was going on, undoubtedly going through her own moments of confusion.

My mother could not speak and my father tried to be cool, nonchalant even. "Heating with wood," he said. "Funny, I never took you for the biofuel type."

"Well, a man's gotta do what a man's gotta do," I said, trying not to cry.

"Is everything okay?" my mother asked.

"Yeah, Mom. Things are good," I said.

She looked at Christine and walked over to her. Christine did not walk away and I don't know what they said to each other but my mother must have said something kind to her.

"Bit of a hike," my dad said.

"How did you find us?"

"Wasn't easy. Kind of a detective story, really. Started with the guy at the gas station."

"Oh, right. Him. Sweet fella."

"Salt of the earth. He wanted to know what crime you were wanted for."

"I hope you told him I was a mass murderer."

"I would have said that if I could have thought of it at the time. But he gave me a couple of clues. Then I started asking around about camps and cabins. This is the fourth place we checked. You didn't exactly pick the Hilton." But it wasn't an insult.

"We wanted to keep things simple," I said.

My dad saw the copy of *Walden* sitting on a log nearby and smiled, shook his head. "Never thought you'd be into this back to the land stuff."

"Me neither," I said. I swallowed hard. "You guys okay?" I asked.

"We are now. Your mother was pretty worried. Me too. When you called we at least knew you were alive. Thanks for that, by the way." It was pretty weird how they weren't angry as hell at me. My guess is they had planned this out. They had decided to be cool. No big lectures. No screaming. No threat of punishment of any kind. I think this made me feel even more guilty for hurting them so much.

"Why are you thanking me?"

"Because you called. Because you were thinking of us. You knew we would be scared sick."

"It was Christine's idea to call," I said, nodding towards her.

"She okay?"

"I think so."

"What do we do now?" he asked.

"I'm not sure."

Christine seemed kind of quiet but not nearly as freaked out as I thought she'd be. We all sat down inside and I made a fire and boiled some water for tea. Christine offered my parents some chapatti bread and they ate it as if they were at communion in a church.

As they left, my dad left us his cell phone and an extra battery. Whatever came next was up to us.

• • •

"They said I could live at your house if I wanted," Christine told me after my parents put on their backpacks and headed on their return hike to Harborville. "Your mom said I could stay in her sewing room."

"Her sewing room?"

"That's what she called it."

"I don't know," I said. It all sounded too incredibly weird. And then a profound sadness settled over both of us. We had to come face to face with the fact that this difficult but incredible experience we were sharing would inevitably come to an end. It would sound appropriate to say we were living in a fantasy world but we were not. It had been more real than anything that I had lived in my life. More challenging, more intense, more "deliberate." As Thoreau would say, "Children, who play life, discern its true laws and relations more clearly than men who fail to live it worthily . . ."

• • •

When the time came, Christine and I hiked out of there, leaving the cabin neat and cleaned and with a note apologizing about the busted lock. We hiked through the cool green generosity of the forest and down the road to the gas station by the road on what turned out to be a Thursday. There was even a date for it on a calendar.

My dad was waiting for us in his car. My mom was there with him and she said we were both looking "healthy."

"How's Ben?" I asked.

"His grades are slipping. Think it's too much sports," my dad said. "Aside from that he seems to be doing fine. He keeps asking about you."

"Did you hear any more from the school?"

"Dr. Cromwell was pretty upset about you disappearing. But he said he had faith in you. He called several times. I told him about our visit."

"What about Farnsworth?"

"It's not going to reopen this year. Cromwell said he

wouldn't give up on it, though. He calls it his life's work."

"He's crazy," I said.

"Crazy in a good way," my mom said, and then she added, "The world needs crazy sometimes."

Christine sat silently for the hour-long drive back to my home, except for the monosyllabic answers she gave to my parents' questions about what she liked to eat and what kind of music she listened to. But they were polite enough to not ask any truly personal questions.

• • •

To say that my new life back at home was weird would be an understatement. Christine genuinely liked my mother and my mother liked her. Both my parents treated her with respect and kindness. Ben didn't know what to make of her and mostly steered a path out of her way. She moved into the "sewing room" where there was a bed beside the expensive sewing machine that my mother almost never used. Awkward is one way to describe bathroom sharing and the general bumping into each other around the house. We spent too much time watching television and not talking to each other except for when we'd go for a walk in the suburban neighborhood.

My mother, I think, held her breath each time we went out, half-expecting perhaps that we'd never come back in through the front door. Instead of saying something that she was really feeling, my mom would say something about being sure to be back in time for dinner.

The fact that my parents were willing to take me back without any punishment and the fact they were willing to take Christine in while asking very few questions dramatically changed the way I saw my folks. Maybe they had each always been that kind of open-minded adult and I'd never seen it.

Or maybe they'd changed.

Maybe we'd all changed.

But Christine and I were no longer living our life of Thoreau in the woods. And that had changed both of us in some other way. We talked about our experience sometimes as we walked through the neighborhood. What we had lived together. What we had felt.

And now things were so different. We were both "adjusting" to our new situation.

If Cromwell could not come up with a way to reopen Farnsworth, my parents thought I should "give the public school system another shot." My mom wondered out loud if Christine might consider the same. "We'd be willing to hire tutors for both of you," my mom said.

And there was something about the way that she said that which made me realize that, in her own way, my mom was willing to accept Christine as a kind of daughter. By now she had seen the scars, had sat down for a heart-to-heart with Christine and absorbed the tragic tale that was her life. And my parents had taken all of that in their stride.

But there was something else, too. I was going through this big identity change. I had lost my anger. The world was still an unfair, totally fucked-up place as far as I was concerned, but I didn't hate all of it. I now understood that this world still held some . . . some real possibilities, for Christine and for me. I just didn't know what to do next.

Chapter Twenty-six

My brother Ben got kicked off the wrestling team for taking some kind of pills before a match. His only defense was, he said, that everyone was doing it, but he was the one who got caught. After that, he must have started to act up in classes because he had this chip on his shoulder the size of a basketball. That got him suspended.

My perfect brother was not so perfect after all.

My mother and Christine had become . . . well, friends. It was spooky. Christine helped her with meals sometimes and they watched some afternoon talk shows in the living room. There was talk of them taking a computer course together.

I spent way too much time alone in my room drifting back into old dead spaces I had once inhabited. I listened to music, I watched some bad TV. I read a book about the United States Marine Corps Paris Island training program where the men chanted at the top of their lungs that they were "highly motivated, truly dedicated, rompin', stompin', bloodthirsty, kill-crazy United States Marine Corps recruits, sir!" And I wondered what it would be like to be a soldier there.

Christine and I were strangely shy around each other these days, drifting in our own directions. On those long walks together down the sidewalks of the town, we tried to reconnect and we talked about our time at the cabin but, as soon as the words were spoken, everything about those sweet days together seemed impossibly long ago and far away. One day when no one else was home, Christine came into my room and lay down beside me on the bed. She didn't say anything at all and I held her in my arms. I held her tightly and I listened to her breathe. I felt her breath on my neck. And I almost told her that I loved her.

But I didn't.

• • •

I was growing frustrated and restless around the house. I told my mom that I wanted her to drive me back to Harborville to visit Doctor Cromwell and she thought that was a great idea. Christine said she wanted to come too so she could check in at the post office and see if there was any mail for her. We listened to alternative music all the way there and my mom was cool about it all. She dropped Christine downtown and drove me to where Dr. C. was living now that the school was closed.

"I'll walk back to town when I'm done here and meet you somewhere in two hours," I said.

"Sure, I've got some shopping to do. Then I'll go to Alfredo's and have a coffee. I'll be there waiting for you."

"See you then."

• • •

It was a big old Victorian house that been divided up into small apartments. I rang the buzzer for Cromwell, the door clicked, and I opened it. The hallway was messy and there was a distinct smell of stale piss in the stairway—cat or human, I wasn't sure which. Outside one apartment were a couple of bags of garbage and a small oddly-stacked pile of beer bottles. I went up the stairs to the third floor and knocked on 3F.

At first I didn't recognize the guy who answered.

"Carson," said the man in old faded jeans and flannel shirt. No robe, no corny academic hat, a day's growth of hair on his jaws and a surprising look of weariness on his face.

"Dr. C.," I said.

"Come in."

I walked in and looked around at the messy room with its old faded furniture and newspapers scattered about. An empty pizza box. A musty smell to the place. I sat down on an uncomfortable, straight-back chair.

"How are things?" Doc asked, collating some pages of newsprint and folding them back together.

"I miss the school," I said.

"So do I. Not much we can do about that right now."

"What happened to Ryan?"

He waved a hand in the air and laughed. "His father's lawyers have these local people all tied up in knots. Ryan will probably be a grandfather before it ever goes to court. But you, what about you?"

I told him about the cabin in the woods. About Christine.

"I felt . . . um . . . betrayed, you know?" Dr. Cromwell said. "We didn't know what happened to you."

"What did you think?"

He threw his hands up. "Some people thought you'd do something stupid, you know, really stupid. But I knew better. I knew that whatever you had decided to do, you had your reasons for doing it and that you were okay. I told your parents that. I told everyone that."

"You had faith in me even after I split?"

"I was just hurt that you didn't trust me enough to tell me."

"There wasn't much to tell. I didn't have a plan."

He let out a small, defeated laugh. "Oh, well, things turned okay, did they?"

"I don't know," I said.

"The girl?"

"She's great. We had this amazing thing . . ."

"Had? You said *had*. Past tense."

I had said it without thinking. "Well, she's living at my house."

"Oh boy," he said. "And your folks are okay with this?"

"It's not quite like that."

"You're full of surprises."

I let out a lungful of air. "I'm full of confusion is what I'm full of. I'm tired of being confused all the time. When do I get over that?" He was a shrink after all and that was partly why I was here. I wanted to know what the hell I was going through. I wanted a name for it.

"It ends when you die, which in your case, is going to be many decades from now. Sorry, my friend, that's the way it works."

"I liked it better when I was angry all the time."

"Think of it as evolution, Carson. You get born. You get pissed off. You find something, something that changes your life in a profound way. Then it slips away even while you're holding onto it. Yeah, and then you feel a sense of loss and—your word—confusion."

"And then you die," I said, summing up the plotline that was supposed to be my life.

"It rather sucks, doesn't it?" he said.

I wasn't used to hearing him talk like this.

"You've been hanging around screwed-up kids too long," I said. "You need to get out of the house more often."

"What do you advise? Run off to a cabin in the woods?"

I laughed. "What about Farnsworth?"

Hands in the air again. "Some of the parents are helping me. We're looking around for a new facility. It may take quite a while. A lot of people in the town here don't want us to reopen. Ryan's stash was just what they were hoping for. A reason to close us down."

"But you're not giving up?"

"'The spirit burning unbent, may writhe, rebel—the weak alone, repent.' William Wordsworth."

"Meaning you'll find a way, right?"

"Meaning I'll try." But right then Cromwell looked to be anything but a man determined to succeed. I wondered how much scrubbing it would take to clean off the graffiti on his brow that said "Loser" in big bold letters.

Chapter Twenty-seven

I sighed heavily as I walked out of the apartment building and headed downtown. I was walking by the IGA store on Main Street and looked in through the windows. Christine was standing there talking to the cashier at one of the checkout lines. I sat down on a bench to wait for her to come out and studied the pigeons walking around in their crazy circles on the sidewalks, picking at scraps of food and cigarette butts. Somewhere I had read that pigeons ate cigarette butts and became addicted to nicotine. Another noble accomplishment of the human species.

When I looked in the window again, she was still talking to the cashier, a truly frazzled looking woman about the age of my mother. The pigeons had flown off and I was just a bored kid sitting on a bench, so I decided to go in and tell Christine I was here.

As I walked in, the cashier was talking to her boss, a man I'd noticed around town before with a perpetual scowl on his face, the look someone had if he'd just stepped in dog shit. The boss nodded and the cashier was taking off her apron and locking her cash register. She and Christine were both walking my way when Christine noticed me.

"Carson," she said, surprised to see me. They both stopped in their tracks. The woman was giving me a thorough once-over in a nervous sort of way.

"Carson," Christine continued, "this is my mother."

At first, I don't think it registered. I stood silently.

"Hi," I said, stunned.

"Hi," she said and then, turning to Christine, added, "He's tall, isn't he?" as if I wasn't even there.

We were in the way. Shoppers were trying to angle their carts around us on their way to the parking lot. "Guess we're blocking traffic," Christine's mom said.

"Listen," Christine said to her mom. "You go back to work. I'll come back later."

Her mom looked at me warily and twisted her hands together. "Sure, honey," she finally said. "I'll be here." And she hugged her daughter to her.

Outside, Christine seemed nervous and unsettled. "Walk with me," she said and she led me down to the harbor where we walked to the end of the wharf.

"I thought you said she was gone."

"She was. Now she's back. She said she didn't know that she was behind on the rent on the trailer. She said she was sorry."

I was having a hard time reading the look on Christine's face. Some kind of war was going on in her head. We both looked down into the dark, clear water. Nearby, fishing boats bobbed slightly at their moorings. "Tide's high," I said. "The moon's on our side of the planet."

She touched my cheek then and made me look at her but

I couldn't keep eye contact. And then she kissed me and I put my arms around her and pulled her to me.

While I was still holding her she told me, "She wants me to move back in with her. She says she can't afford to pay the rent where she's at. She can't afford to live there alone. And she says they need another cashier at the IGA. She can get me the job."

I felt myself slipping away, as if I were being pulled upward into the sky, up to that invisible moon that had filled the harbor with this tide. "What are you going to do?"

I tried to let go of her so I could look her in the face but she wouldn't let me. She buried her face in my shoulder and took a deep breath. "I'm going to move back with her."

"But I thought you told me how unreliable she is . . . about how badly you were treated growing up. About the times she left you. What about all that?"

"I know. I know."

"Then why?"

"Because she's still my mother."

When we walked into Alfredo's a half hour later, the indignant waiter, the guy who had told me I wasn't wanted in town, gave us a dirty look. But I saw my mom sitting by the window and we walked over there without saying a word to anyone. She paid her bill and we left Harborville. And it was a long, quiet drive back home. My mother tried to muster a conversation but neither Christine nor I were in the mood for talking.

• • •

I somehow graduated from public high school. In truth, I don't think I really passed but the principal was a practical man who realized that some of his faculty members would express great displeasure (and possibly quit) if they discovered I had returned for one more year of mutual torture.

My parents made a noble effort at trying to convince me to go to university and, failing that, community college, but I'd had my share of sitting in classrooms, thank you.

The summer of my so-called graduation was a kind of plateau. I made little effort to do anything and could not find enthusiasm for any new occupation of my time. I recall that I ate three meals a day at the urging of my mom, and my dad thought he could wake me up by introducing me to some of his favorite books by what he called "friends of your ole buddy Thoreau." There were Ralph Waldo Emerson and Walt Whitman in particular. Then he tried a more modern writer—Farley Mowat. But I decided I didn't have any real passion for philosophy or poetry or modern books about nature.

I was shocked one sleepy July afternoon to get a call from Fin who was phoning to tell me he'd been accepted at a university in New England. He was going to major in physics, of course. I asked him if he still hoped to build a nuclear weapon and he just laughed. "I was a pretty sick adolescent," he said. "I think I'm over that now." He sounded totally different from the old Fin I knew. He sounded more mature, for one thing, and confident. "What about you, Carson? What are your future plans?"

"I don't know, Fin. I really don't."

"Keeping your options open, eh?"

"Something like that."

• • •

In mid-August, I got another out-of-the-blue phone call, this one from Dr. Cromwell. He'd found a new home for Farnsworth Academy. The grandparents of a former student had died and left a big chunk of cash to the school, plus a farm outside of Harborville. There was a big old house and a couple of buildings, one of which he hoped to convert into classrooms.

"I want you to work for me," Cromwell said.

"What kind of work?"

"Well, there's a lot that needs to be done here at the new school—landscaping maybe, fixing things, construction. You're good with your hands, right? But I was also thinking you might be somebody who would be helpful to the new students, too."

"I don't mind the physical work but . . . um . . . I'm not sure how I can be of much help with your students. You might recall that I'm not really all that good with people."

"I wouldn't worry about that," Cromwell said in a serious tone. "We can work on your social graces when you get here. What do you say?"

• • •

And so I said yes. I moved there by the end of that week and, under the direction of a local carpenter, I learned about tools and construction and got to know what it felt like to go to bed with sore muscles, blisters on my thumbs, and calluses on my palms.

There were only a few students at first and some of them gave me a hard time. I had watched the new students arrive in September, each with the heavy baggage of an unhappy childhood. Some were tortured souls, some were mean.

Some appeared so damaged that it was hard to look them in the face. But Cromwell explained to me how to show respect for them. And he told me that I could train myself to be helpful to them if I looked beyond all the damage and hurt to envision them as older, happier, even successful individuals. I had to believe that anyone, absolutely anyone, could be healed.

Once the major cleanup and the construction were finished, I stayed on to become the maintenance man. The janitor. It was my idea. I wanted the job. I wanted a place in the world doing something that mattered.

• • •

After she had moved out of my house, I talked to Christine on the phone often but it was always uncomfortable. I had tried to visit her but she was working long hours, and when she wasn't working she said she was too tired to do anything.

Once I was back living near Harborville, I could visit Christine at her apartment, trying to time it so that I was not there when her mother was home. Her mother had a new boyfriend and sometimes went away with him for the weekend. Sometimes for a week. Her mother had lost her cashier job at the IGA but Christine stayed on. And she worked a second job in the evenings at a drugstore to be able to keep up the rent.

We were shy and awkward around each other and promised over and over that we'd remain friends, that we'd be there for each other no matter what happened. But we knew that whatever it was we had lost could never be retrieved. Sometimes I would go into town and watch her through the window of the IGA or at the drugstore. Sometimes I would just walk in and say, "I was just passing through so I thought I'd stop and say hi." She'd smile and thank me for doing this. Other times, I would just watch her from a distance and not go in at all. I just wanted to assure myself that she was all right. And then I'd walk on by, maybe sit for a time on the wharf above the harbor or just return to the school feeling a bit sad, a bit foolish.

That November, Christine and I walked out to the cabin together, retracing our steps on that long, beautiful hike out of town along the inlet. There were long moments of awkward silence between us as we tried to reconnect.

"I still think a lot about you," she said.

"And I think about you."

"But everything is different, isn't it?"

"Yeah, it is," I said. "But I don't know why."

"We both had to move on. It's like we didn't have a choice."

"But I don't understand how it happened."

"Neither do I. It just did."

"Do you remember the stars?" I asked.

"I can still see them when I close my eyes," Christine said and I touched her hand just then. I brought it up to my mouth and kissed it. We stopped walking and stood like that along the banks of the inlet for a minute, maybe more. We both had our eyes closed and had returned to the past.

After that, neither one of us could find anything to say to the other. We walked on, hoping, I guess, that when we arrived at the cabin, we would have somehow actually delivered ourselves back to that amazing time.

As we neared the cabin, however, we heard gunshots and when we got closer, we heard men laughing and then saw them sitting around outside in camouflage clothing, shotguns propped alongside of them. They were laughing and drinking beer and we saw nearly a dozen geese hanging upside down from a tree branch, tied there with string as the blood dripped out of their bodies onto the ground.

We turned and left and knew we'd never come back this way again.

• • •

Now, on the darkest of nights, I walk outside the new academy farmhouse after all the students are in their respective rooms. I walk out into the fields and look up into the clear night sky. I watch for the meandering satellites and I trace the Milky Way and I name the constellations silently to myself. And sometimes I find that I open my mouth and I say her name out loud. *Christine.* And once I've said her name out loud I want to go to her.

But, instead, I breathe in the cold, clear night air. I take it deep into my lungs and I remind myself that there are good things in this world you can hold onto, important things that stay inside you and never go away. Even though the world has moved on and everything has changed forever.

Lesley has taught at Dalhousie University for the past twenty-five years. He is the author of over sixty books for adults and kids. His young adult novels explore diverse topics from skateboarding and surfing to racism and environmental issues. Lesley surfs year-round in the North Atlantic and is considered the father of transcendental wood-splitting. He's worked as a rehab counsellor, a freight hauler, a corn farmer, a janitor, a journalist, a lead guitarist, a newspaper boy, and even a well-digger. He lives in a 200-year-old farmhouse at Lawrencetown Beach where he runs Pottersfield Press.

Choyce also hosts a nationally syndicated TV talk show on BookTelevision. His novel, *The Republic of Nothing*, is currently being developed as a feature length movie. In 2002, Goose Lane Editions published Choyce's circumferential history book, *The Coasts of Canada*. That same year, his animal epic film *The Skunk Whisperer* was broadcast across Canada and heralded at the Maine International Film Festival. With the Surf Poets, he has released two poetry/music albums, *Long Lost Planet* and *Sea Level*.

Book excerpts, music and links to videos can be found at www.lesleychoyce.com.